THE
SOLITARY
CHILD

and Other Short Stories

by

Chalfont St. Giles

ISBN: 979-8-88683-625-7
eISBN: 979-8-88683-626-4

DORRANCE
PUBLISHING CO
EST. 1920
PITTSBURGH, PENNSYLVANIA 15238

To my Fruhling family, with gratitude

Table of Contents

THE HEIRS

Marjorie knew the exact moment when Maury's daughters opened her letter. Her cell pinged and lit up with over-the-top gushing affirmations of affection.

Some Ancestry websites had led him to Marjorie, and Maury had sent a picture of his three daughters, their spouses and their children. None seemed to be doing well. Factories had closed, the husbands' skills were obsolete.

"The kids don't come round much because I can't give them any money," Maury wrote Marjorie. "They just come to squabble over their mother's things."

Marjorie was disappointed that Maury's daughters did not immediately reach out to their newfound relative, but she told herself they are busy with their families. Her intense loneliness was nevertheless replaced by the joy of suddenly belonging to a family.

She wrote Maury, "Just give me the name of your solicitor, don't tell the girls, but I will help them!" She handwrote a neat list of cash bequests to go to each daughter, and put it in the mail to Maury, and then she called Maury's solicitor. It was he, not the daughters, who told her that Maury had just passed away.

Almost staggering with exhaustion after a 17-hour flight, Marjorie gamely took a taxi straight to the church. The main funeral service was over, but she made it in time for the short ceremony to lower Maury into the ground. The family was sitting under a broad canopy on one side of the coffin. Marjorie recognized each of them from the photo Maury sent her.

She approached them eagerly, stumbling and almost falling on the uneven, muddy grass. Maury's daughters looked at her stonily, and after too long a pause, someone said, "You alright, hmmm?" The tone was flat, the words motivated more by convention than concern.

The grandchildren squirmed in their chairs and stared at her, their little faces mirroring their parents' guarded expressions. Marjorie tried to make a connection. She said to a small boy, "You must be James. My son's name was James, he'd have been your fourth cousin." James' mother immediately found it necessary to start a conversation with the person behind her. So Marjorie handed a card with her cellphone number to James. "Give this to your mum, there's a good boy."

The clergyman adjusted his umbrella, and started to speak, and all eyes swiveled to him. Marjorie went to join the mourners standing in the rain. Even though the prayers and readings were blessedly short because of the rain, her legs just gave out and she plopped down on her suitcase. The clergyman ended on a note of hope that they would see their loved-one again in the hereafter, and the daughters busily adjusted the children's coats. They ignored Marjorie. When little James raised his hand to wave good-bye, his mother quickly slapped it down. Nobody wanted to be bothered with this doddering old relative who talked funny, sat on a suitcase at a funeral, and didn't know how to dress for English weather. Marjorie watched them disappear into the drizzly mist. Never had she felt more alone.

She took the bus to her hotel. Cold wind and rain lashed the windows day and night, and every bone in her body ached. She kept her cell phone handy, but there was never a call, message or email. One morning she got out of bed, booked a flight, paid her hotel bill, and went home.

Stepping out of the plane in Brisbane was like stepping into a hot blast furnace. She leaned out of the taxi window all the way home. The cat twisted himself around her legs and Billabong's toothless grin stretched from ear to ear as he carried her suitcase into the house.

Billabong lived in the aborigine camp down by the eucalyptus grove. Back when Marjorie and Tom were still struggling to get the farm going, Billabong had just shown up one day. His real name was Tjandamurra, but the farmers all called him Billabong. Tom was irritated at first with him hanging around, but soon realized he needed him to supervise the Islanders who cut the cane. Billabong had been with them ever since. When the cat killed rats, he buried them, when Marjorie squealed at insects in the cupboards, he caught them, and when snakes found a home under the house, Billabong was there to relocate them. He plucked slimy bodies off Marjorie's door screens and tried to stop the cutters from playing football with the cane toads. With his help, the farm prospered, and Tom hired a housekeeper to give Marjorie some free time. She set up a school and bribed the aborigine camp children with sweets to come sit on the verandah and learn their ABCs. She wanted to give the little ones a head start for town school; lord knows they already had enough stacked against them. This got Tom quite a vicious ribbing from his conservative friends at the Watering Hole, so much so that it affected his darts game.

When Baby James was fretful, Billabong sent his girls to rock and soothe him, so Marjorie could have some rest. When Baby James died, Tom took his grief to the

Watering Hole, leaving Marjorie alone. Billabong came and stood vigil on the verandah. He sang the songs of his ancestors, a mourning lament as heartfelt as if he had lost a child of his own. Voices from the camp wafted up and joined his, and their soulful keening comforted Marjorie and honored Baby James on his final journey.

Eventually Tom's heart gave out, and the neighboring farmer quickly offered a good price to annex the property. With Tom gone, Marjorie was desperately lonely. By now Billabong was scrawny and bent, with sunken eyes and a white grizzled beard, and she worried this year would be his last. Then cousin Maury found her. Suddenly she came alive, picturing herself selling up and moving to England, and happily living in the bosom of her loving new family. The cane was already burned off and the harvest well under way when Maury's solicitor gave her the bad news. That's when Marjorie quickly made arrangements to leave. She had noticed Billabong's gloomy face and reassured him.

"I'm just going on a little walk-about."

"Yes, Mum," he said, as he put her bag in the taxi.

Marjorie had been back two months to the day, when she was jarred out of a deep sleep. Her phone had buzzed urgently and lit up like a Christmas tree. That was probably when the daughters got around to sorting through Maury's belongings and had opened her bequest letter. The air was thick with the sticky heat, a sour odor rose from the burned fields, and flies bumped mindlessly against the windowpanes. Marjorie sat on the porch re-reading Maury's daughters' effusive messages. The decision she would have to make sent tears tumbling silently down her cheeks.

A VERY GOOD MAN

Heat spirals danced off the blacktop, and to the east, hills like golden breasts covered the miles to the oak-studded foothills. Every evening, the east-west mountains funnel cool Pacific Ocean breezes into our valley. The hot sunny days and crisp nights are ideal for grape-growing, and tourists flock to the local wineries. My parents weren't in the wine business, but they owned a horse ranch that catered to those tourists, offering pleasant rides beside the rustic Santa Ynez River. I have photo albums filled with pictures of smiling holidaymakers making like cowboys on their Appaloosas. I longed to revive the family business and be part of the local Western culture. The abundance of sun-drenched days and mild temperatures all year long made it a delight to be outdoors, very different to the humid summers and cold blustery winters I endured in New York.

The narrow ribbon of road passed several ranches. It was late afternoon when I turned in to the driveway. I craned my neck as I passed the caretaker's cottage. The door was open but there was no sign of Jorge. My parents liked Jorge, they said he was a very good man, and allowed him to live in the cottage rent-free. In exchange he mended the paddock fences and kept weeds at bay. He earned cash feeding horses for absentee ranch owners, and he got some of his meals free at the church. My parents often joked that he probably had more money than they did. It's been several months since they were laid to rest in serene Oak Hill cemetery. My marketing job with a New York publisher tied me to a contract, and it took a while to untangle myself from East Coast life and obligations. And a messy breakup, which lingered only because my ex showed sudden renewed interest in me when word got to him, via mutual friends, that I had inherited a ranch in California. Through all of that, though, it did give me some peace of mind to know that Jorge was watching the ranch until I could move here.

My car bounced jarringly on the deep driveway ruts. For a horse riding in a trailer, it would be like being churned in a cement mixer. My parents had sold all their horses, and I had persuaded a local paving contractor to meet me here today to discuss grading before I bought any of my own. I was surprised to hear music as I approached the house, a mariachi band so loud that it drowned out the crunch of my tires on the gravel. The first shock was to see seven kids of varying sizes splashing in the pool, their boom box resting on a nearby lounge chair. The biggest of them was a stocky youth of about sixteen.

Jorge's battered pickup partially blocked the open front door. I stepped up on the porch and got the second shock. Two large women filled the kitchen, shouting to each other as they clattered spoons in mixing bowls. Beyond them, I caught a glimpse of two pairs of pointy-toed cowboy boots resting on the coffee table, and disembodied hands clutching beer cans. The crowd noise of a televised soccer game mingled with the two women's laughter. I knocked politely. No-one noticed me. It was only when a small wet child burst in shouting, "Mama, mama! *Francisco me empjo*, he hit me!" that the women looked toward the door. Their mouths fell open, cooking utensils poised, directing their gaze not at the complaining child, but at me. Neither woman spoke. The absence of their kitchen noise must have caught the attention of the two men, and in a sudden flurry one of them leapt off the couch and bolted out the side door. I could see him running as fast as he could up the driveway. It was the caretaker, Jorge.

The child standing in the wet puddle continued to whine but was ignored by the women. They were looking at me. Just then the grading contractor drove up. He knocked and stepped into the kitchen behind me.

"Hello, I'm Carlos Garcia, nice to meet you."

He stuck out his hand to me with a wide ingratiating smile. I was still in shock and didn't move. So he stuck out his hand to the nearest of the two women. She reached forward and shook it. He then looked over at the skinny man craning forward from the living room couch and waved to him. "*Buenas dias …*"

It became a stop-motion tableau. Nobody moved. Everybody was looking at me.

Finally, I said, "Who are you? What are you doing here?" Neither woman spoke.

The child leaning against the door jamb said, "They don't speak English. We live here."

I said, "What do you mean you live here? For how long?"

The child shrugged. "About six months. Or maybe more. This is our house."

Visions of vicious protracted lawsuits crowded into my head, ownership disputes, fake deeds, garbled titles, heavy legal fees.

I said slowly and clearly, "This house belonged to my parents. I inherited it and I own it now."

The child translated for the women, and then corrected me. "It's Jorge's house." He went back to the pool.

Just then my cell buzzed. It was my ex, Paul.

"I can't talk now," I said quickly.

"Well, I just wanted to know how you're doing." His voice was schmoozy. "We should talk. You know …"

"I can't talk now, Paul."

The contractor was easing toward the door. "I guess you folks better decide …"

I snapped, "Stay!" The contractor paused mid-step.

"Oh, Babe, you know I'll stay …"

"Not you, Paul. I have to go." I hung up.

The largest woman spat out a few words. Mr. Garcia translated. "She says it's Jorge's house." I beckoned to the contractor. He followed docilely as I trudged up the rough track to the cottage by the gate.

"Jorge!" I shouted. The door was closed now, so I knew he was in there. "Jorge!" I shouted again. No answer. I motioned to Mr. Garcia to go in the front, and I raced around to the back, and caught Jorge sidling out. The contractor stood his ground. Jorge looked from one to the other of us, and then down at his feet.

"What's going on, Jorge," I said. "Who are all these people?" His English failed him, and he mumbled something I didn't understand.

The contractor filled me in. "He said they're just friends visiting."

The room darkened and a shadow filled the doorway. The larger of the two women heaved in breathlessly. Jorge dodged behind Mr. Garcia. Mr. Garcia began rapid-fire interpretation for me, his head swiveling from one to the other.

The woman bellowed, "Jorge, you said you own this ranch, right?" Her hands were on her hips, feet planted wide.

"Well, I live here." Jorge shut his eyes, trying to make it all go away.

"But you do own it, right?"

Mr. Garcia translated, and waited.

"Well, I lived here a long time," Jorge mumbled.

The woman made a loud, exasperated Tsk! "I came up here because you told me you owned a ranch, that you was rich."

"Well, I was lonely, and you wouldn't have come otherwise, and maybe owning the ranch part was not true, but I do have some money …" Jorge finished lamely. He turned red eyes toward me and switched to English. "They can stay in here with me, yes?"

I felt badly for him, but I said, "No they can't, it's too small. Eleven people cannot live here, Jorge, be reasonable. It's only one room."

Jorge brushed the back of his hand across his nose, sniffling. "I didn't think you would mind if Maria came up here to stay with me." He spread his hands. "She's from my hometown. But I didn't know she had three children. Or that her sister and her sister's boyfriend and all their children would be coming too."

Maria started to shriek at me, waving her arms. The contractor didn't bother to translate, and he didn't need to. I got the gist, and it wasn't pretty.

I shook my head, and said to her firmly, "I'm sorry, but you have to go."

Maria didn't need a translation either. She began to wail shrilly, beating her breast.

I tried again. "Jorge, will you please tell her they have to leave."

"Tomorrow?" he said, avoiding eye contact.

"No, today, now," I said. "I am sorry, but I need to move into my house. And I need to discuss road repairs with Mr. Garcia."

"Oh, that's OK," the contractor said quickly. "I can come another time …"

I glared at him, and he closed his mouth. He was the only person in my corner, albeit unwillingly. Nobody said anything. I took out my cell. "I am going to have to call the police …"

Before I could dial, my phone jangled. It was Paul again.

"I can't talk now." I told him.

"Well, I was worried about you. You sounded a bit tense. If you want to talk … we should really talk …"

"I can't right now, Paul. Another time, OK?" I hung up and started to dial. "Look, I am calling the police, see, I am calling the police."

Maria shot me a dirty look and turned and marched back down the driveway toward the house. I hung up without completing the call. I followed Maria down the driveway, leaving Jorge standing forlornly in the cottage. Mr. Garcia followed me. I think by now he was feeling invested in the drama, sensing some responsibility for the outcome.

Back in the kitchen, both women began sullenly tossing dishes of food into plastic bags and emptying the cupboards, heaving boxes of cereal and sacks of rice, flour, and sugar into Hefty bags. They pulled armfuls of clothes and shoes from the closets and threw everything into the back of Jorge's truck. The women herded the wet bodies wrapped in my parents' towels, their angry eyes accusing me, look how cruel you are, making little children cry. The skinny boyfriend wandered out with a beer in his hand and stood watching.

The oldest boy stubbornly refused to leave. Maria called to him, "Francisco!" Scowling, he pulled down his shorts and peed into the pool, and then defiantly kicked both lounge chairs into the water.

I watched as they rattled up the driveway, but instead of continuing out the gate as I expected, the truck stopped at the cottage. They began to unload and take bags inside. I raced back up the driveway, the contractor close on my heels.

I could hardly catch my breath. "Jorge, they cannot move in here. I told you, it is not big enough for eleven people."

The two women ignored me and continued to carry Hefty bags into the cottage.

Jorge mumbled in his own defense, "You can see I am not helping them."

So, I called the police again, and this time I let it ring, holding up my cell so they could see. I hoped it would halt their unloading.

It didn't.

"What is the nature of your emergency." I told the dispatcher some people had moved into my house. She put me through to somebody. After a long pause, another woman came on the line. "Yes?" I repeated what I had told the dispatcher. She said sharply, "You can't just throw them out. Did you give them notice? There's a process. You need to give them notice in all the appropriate languages. Tenants have rights, you know. An eviction can take up to a year."

The two women smirked at my frustration as I argued on the phone, and they defiantly went into the cottage. They all looked so uncomfortable, eleven people squeezed into that tiny room, standing jammed together as tight as asparagus stalks in a can. They clearly had no plans to leave.

Just then my phone rang. I hoped it was the police calling back. It was Paul.

"When would be a good time to talk? We need to clear the air between us, Babe …"

"Oh, yes, hi, OK, in an hour?" I disconnected Paul but kept the phone pressed close to my ear and began talking loudly and forcefully, as though I actually had someone on the line who would come and do something. "Oh, OK, so you can help them to move out in an hour? That would be great!"

The women looked at each other uncertainly. Francisco suddenly punched his fist through a windowpane. Jorge flinched. He reluctantly took out his cell phone. After a while he said something to Maria. The contractor translated; they were being given shelter at the church.

To my surprise, a patrol car rolled up and parked just outside the gate. Maria spotted it, and she and the other woman quickly began to reload the Hefty bags into Jorge's pickup. They also loaded the cottage furniture. The table, chairs, the rug, everything from the cottage went into the truck bed.

I looked at Jorge. "Do they know the furniture belongs to the cottage?" Jorge looked off into the distance, pretending not to hear. I let it go because Francisco was also looking at Jorge. Jorge barely reached Francisco's shoulder, and he seemed to shrink even smaller under Francisco's angry glare. He looked so miserable that I said quickly, "You can come back here anytime, Jorge, you will always have a home here."

The police presence seemed to galvanize the women, and they hastily got in the pickup next to Francisco, who was now at the wheel. The other kids and the skinny boyfriend hunkered down amongst the furniture in the truck bed. Jorge hesitated, as though he wanted to get something else from the cottage. But the truck was already moving, so he hopped in the back.

The police officer probably felt that he had done his job and drove away.

The contractor watched them all leave. He said to me, "Well, it's almost dark."

I said, "Can you come back tomorrow, Mr. Garcia?"

"Um, I'll look at my calendar," he said.

I spent the next couple of hours cleaning my parents' kitchen and living room and stripping the beds. While the dishwasher and laundry machines hummed, I wandered back up to the cottage in the moonlight, too wired by the day's events to go to bed. Cupboard doors stood open revealing bare shelves. All that remained were the curtains moving lazily at the smashed window.

I was standing there in the empty cottage when my phone rang. I saw it was Paul again. My first instinct was to let it go to voicemail. But then I realized that he would keep calling, so reluctantly, I picked up.

"Hi Paul," I said.

"Hi, Babe. You know you used to call me Paulie." His tone was accusing.

I heard the rumble of a truck. It had the distinctive grating sound of Jorge's spare-parts rebuilt engine. It pulled up in front of the cottage, headlights blazing, radio blaring. The furniture was still piled in it. I thought Jorge was bringing it all back.

Relieved to have the distraction, I said to Paul, "Look, I have to go, I need to help my caretaker unload. We can talk tomorrow, OK?" Paul started to say something, but I just said, "Later, OK?" and hung up.

I was about to go out to meet Jorge, but it wasn't Jorge, it was the oldest boy, Francisco, who jumped out of the truck. He seemed unsteady on his feet, and he was talking to himself. I flattened myself against the wall.

Francisco stepped up on the porch, struck a match, and tossed it through the broken window. The curtains flared up immediately with an audible whoosh. I think I heard him laugh. He didn't even close the truck cab door as he rolled down the driveway toward my parents' house. I watched in horror, and then started to run after him. Francisco was already pulling up in front of my open front door when the gas canister that fueled Jorge's cook-stove exploded. Francisco stopped, and for a long moment stared back uncomprehendingly at the cottage. Then in a frenzied grinding of gears and flying gravel, he reversed up the driveway. I had to dive into the bushes, he almost hit me in his haste to get out of there. The old dry wood went up so fast there would have been no chance to save the cottage. Soon all that was left were glowing embers.

I was sitting on the front porch with a cup of coffee. The smell of burned wood hung heavy in the air. My phone rang. It was Paul. I looked at my watch, it was only 6AM, the sun wasn't even up. But of course, in New York Paul's day was well under way.

"Hello, Babe," he said, making his voice sugary sweet. "How are you? I have been so worried about you."

"I'm doing fine, Paul. What do you want to talk about?"

"Well, us. I miss you. I can come out there and give you a hand with the ranch. How big is the ranch? How many horses are you getting? I'd love to learn to ride!"

"What happened to your Upper East Side heiress? You know, the one you left me for."

"Oh, that was just a little fling, it didn't mean anything."

"Well, she obviously didn't think so. She dumped you."

There was a pause while he regrouped.

I heard Jorge's truck arrive. He pulled up in front of the charred ruins of his former home.

"Paul, I have to go. My caretaker just drove up. Look, I think our relationship has run its course. There really isn't anything else to discuss."

"But Babe, I miss you. I can come out there and …"

"Paul, I think this ended while I was still in New York. There's really nothing more to say."

From my porch I could see Jorge pulling up charred floorboards, clawing frantically at the ashes with his bare hands. He was sobbing loudly, his cries echoing across the valley, anguished howls of sheer despair. "*Mi dinero,* my money*, todo mi dinero,* gone."

Paul was saying something. I dropped my phone and began to run up the driveway, but before I could reach him, Jorge's truck was racing out the gate, headed toward town.

It was in the local paper, just a short article. Francisco had always boasted to his schoolmates that his family owned a big horse ranch. To find himself suddenly homeless and living in a church basement was no doubt humiliating for him, more than his pride could bear, but the authorities did not connect him to the fire at the cottage. They reasoned it couldn't be revenge because all Jorge's possessions were safely on his truck, and he didn't even own the cottage. They blamed the faulty cook-stove gas canister.

Francisco claimed to have no idea what had driven a distraught Jorge to seek him out at the church shelter or cause him to futilely pummel the boy's chest with his fists. Francisco retaliated with one punch, and laid Jorge out flat on the floor.

The priest said it was an accident and Maria said it was justifiable self-defense and the church secretary said she hadn't really seen anything. An unconscious Jorge was transported to the hospital and a valiant effort was made to save his life, without success. The church secretary found Maria's family a home as live-in caretakers at a local ranch. They were now my nearest neighbors, and I often heard the faint strains of mariachi music floating across the fields on the evening breeze.

When I placed an ad in the paper for a part-time ranch hand, Francisco showed up on my doorstep to apply for the job. I was staring at him wondering what to say when a pickup lumbered down the driveway, and pulled up at the porch steps. Mr. Garcia got out and tipped his hat to me.

To Francisco he said, *"Hola*! What are you doing here, *mijo?"*

"I want work," said Francisco.

"You want work? I'll give you work; you can help me. Go sit in my truck for a minute, OK?" He turned to me, holding out a piece of paper. "This is an estimate for the grading," he said. "Take a look at it. I can start tomorrow. We can negotiate the price if you're not comfortable."

I handed him a mug of coffee, and he settled into one of the Adirondack porch chairs and gazed out across the pasture.

"You got a beautiful place here," he said. "I knew your folks. Good people."

"Thank you." I nodded. "This looks fine, this is really reasonable, thank you so much. I'll sign it. Thank you for getting going on the job so fast!"

He smiled. "I have an even better surprise for you. I heard you want Appaloosas, right? Like your folks had?" I nodded. "Well, I've found one for you, a real beauty. The owners are selling their ranch. They don't want to sell him to a stranger nobody knows, so I said I would ask you. Interested?"

"Yes!"

"Then let's go meet him! We can walk him down the driveway before the grading begins. If you like him, that is."

I was already on my feet, reaching for my purse.

It was, of course, love at first sight. This beautiful 4-year-old chestnut Appaloosa stood 13 hands high. His spotted coat shone, his hooves had been trimmed, and he had had all his shots. He had clearly been lovingly cared for. His owners said he is gentle, hardworking, and easy to train, all the things that made my parents favor this breed for recreational riders. His owners said "Appie's a very sweet boy," as they gave me his papers and stroked his nose, bidding him a sorrowful goodbye.

Mr. Garcia hauled him in his trailer to my gate, and Francisco took over from there. The horse docilely followed Francisco. Francisco might as well not have held the lead line at all, Appie just simply walked beside him all the way down the driveway to the stable.

"Francisco really has a way with horses," I said to Mr. Garcia. "You've certainly brought out the best in him!"

Mr. Garcia smiled, and said to me, "He just needed some direction. Francisco told me what he did, and he's sorry. To make it right, he will help rebuild the cottage, and his mother Maria will clean for you and cook, she's only asking that while she's working here, the children can use the pool, OK?"

I didn't hesitate. "I need all the help I can get. Deal!"

Early the next day they brought in the grader and they worked through the morning. Maria made burritos for the men. When they took a break, Mr. Garcia came in and sat chatting at the kitchen counter with Maria. The children were splashing happily in the pool. I smiled to myself, it felt good to have them all around.

The afternoon wore on, the men were close to finishing for the day, when a bleating "Hello, hello, hello," came from somewhere near the top of the driveway. It was a familiar voice. I stood up and went to the door, shading my eyes, straining to see who was approaching. Maria and Mr. Garcia joined me on the porch. I had to look twice. It was Paul. He was carefully picking his way across the ruts, trying not to get his tan loafers dirty.

"Hello, surprise, surprise, it's me, Babe!" he said, flailing to keep his balance. He heaved himself and his roller bag up onto the porch and stood dramatically poised there, arms wide.

"Big hug, Babe!" he said breathlessly.

He had on a purple velvet jacket, fashionably skin-tight black pants, a pink shirt, and he carried a black man-bag over his shoulder. He wore his long hair in a man-bun. Maria's jaw dropped, and she stood looking at him as though he belonged somewhere in outer space. My expression must have mirrored hers, but Paul kept on chattering.

"The taxi from the airport wouldn't come down your driveway," Paul was saying. "He made me get out at the gate. I offered him more money to drive me down, but he refused. You've got an awful driveway!" He pointed at the workmen who stood gaping at him. "Babe, it's a good thing you're getting around to fixing it!"

Mr. Garcia mumbled something abrupt and jumped off the porch and went back to work.

The next morning Paul appeared in the doorway of the downstairs bedroom. He was still in his bathrobe, hair spikey and sleep tousled. He yawned and stretched.

I was sitting at the kitchen counter.

"Sleep well?" I asked.

"It was rather lonely down here all by myself." He pecked me on the cheek and eased himself onto a bar stool. "But that will soon change, won't it, Babe? Oh, goody, your cook is here."

Maria put a burrito in front of him. "What's this," he said, warily poking at it with his fork.

"It's a burrito," I told him.

"Ew," he said, screwing up his nose. "Mexican food!" He said to Maria, "I'll have two eggs sunny side up, bacon cooked crispy, and sourdough toast. And coffee."

Maria ignored him and went on cleaning the stove.

Paul said irritably, "She doesn't speak English?" He raised his voice. "I'd like two…"

"Paul, this isn't a restaurant," I said. "Either eat the burrito or I'll make you eggs later."

Paul bit into the burrito and waved it toward the door. "Why are all those people here?"

"They are grading the driveway."

"I can see that. But why are they here so darn early. It's only …" he looked at his watch, "oh, it's 10." He gnawed on the burrito. He said through a mouthful, "So, Babe, shall we go sightseeing today?"

"I'm going to sift through the debris up at the cottage. It burned you know. Maybe there's something salvageable."

"Oh, OK," he said, "Well while you're doing that, I'll go into town and see if I can find a *New York Times*." He stood up and went to the door and nodded toward the workers. "Can one of these people drive me into town?"

Mr. Garcia's men kept on doing what they were doing. No-one looked up.

Something caught Paul's eye. "Is that a horse?" He shaded his eyes, peering at the pasture. "Looks like there's a horse over there."

"Yes, Paul, that's a horse."

"Oh, great. You've actually got one horse! It's a slow start, but at *least* you have *made* a start."

He kissed me on the forehead and disappeared into the bathroom.

I came back from the cottage, my arms full. I had found doorknobs, an iron doorstop, and some hand-painted ceramic tiles. I found Paul sitting on the porch, watching the workers.

"It's so dusty!" he complained.

"It will be until they've finished the grading."

"I asked one of them to hose off the porch, but he ignored me."

"Paul, this isn't a plantation in the south. They don't work for you. They work for Mr. Garcia. Let them get on with it, OK?"

Paul looked moodily toward the horizon. The far-off purple hills were crowned with strands of gold and pearly pink. The breeze languidly stirred the cobalt leaves of the Blue Oak, its silvery bark ghostly white in the afternoon sun.

Paul yawned and said, "What is there to do around here?" I was gazing at the glowing landscape. Paul nudged me. "What do you do for fun around here, Babe? Is there opera?"

"Nope, no opera."

"Oh, no opera. Well, I will miss the opera."

"How often did you go to the opera, Paul?"

"Well, it was *there* if I *wanted* to go, that's the point. You know, you could sell this farm and come back to New York with me. We could get a nice big upper East Side apartment, go to art galleries, Broadway shows, museums, restaurants, just like we used to. You loved doing all that."

"That was then, this is now. I like it here," I said.

"Well, then, of course I want to be where *you* are."

He leaned over, leering with a sultry smile. "Why don't we ..."

"Don't even," I said.

"What?" he said, eyebrows raised innocently. "I was going to say why don't we play cards?"

I stood up. "I'm going over to visit Appie. Want to come?"

Francisco was leaning on the rail feeding the horse some hay. It was a quiet moment both were clearly enjoying.

I said admiringly, "Francisco, you are the true horse whisperer. Appie clearly loves you!"

Paul rushed toward them. "Let me!" he said. He snatched a handful of hay from Francisco and shoved it in the horse's face. Appie reared back, tossing his head to shake off the stalks in his nostrils. The horse came back to the rail. He sought out Francisco and stood quietly beside him. Paul tried again. He ran at the fence. Francisco stepped forward and tried to stop him, but Paul lunged headlong at the horse. Appie abruptly reared his head and pushed Paul hard. Paul went flying. Mr. Garcia's workers stopped what they were doing and just stood looking at the man in the purple velvet jacket lying sprawled in the dirt.

Paul wailed, "It attacked me! Did you see that? The horse attacked me!"

Francisco said, "No, he just didn't want you to step on the snake."

"Oh, he saved me from a snake?" Paul quickly got to his feet.

"No, he saved the snake," Francisco said. He pointed at a little garter.

The next morning there were screams from Paul's bedroom. I don't know where the snake came from, I had never seen snakes in the house before. It was just a little garter. It had somehow found its way into Paul's shoe. Mr. Garcia and Francisco were working nearby, but kept their heads down, though they must have heard.

"Help, help," shrieked Paul.

Finally, Francisco ambled into the house. "What's up?" he said.

"Look, look, a snake," Paul whimpered.

Francisco reached over and picked it up, carried it outside, setting it down gently in the grass, and went back to his work. Early the following evening Paul said he had a headache from the heat. He was about to climb into bed, but there was a big Jerusalem cricket right in the middle of his pillow. He screamed and Maria came and removed it. She shrugged like she had no idea where it came from. Paul spent the night sitting upright in a chair.

Other than the strange sudden appearance of wild creatures in Paul's room, everything was going smoothly. Appie had settled in, and Francisco kept his stall tidy and walked and groomed him daily. The driveway was coming along nicely, and Mr. Garcia started Francisco and two other men on rebuilding the cottage. Maria came every day to clean away the dust and cook, leaving her sister and her sister's skinny boyfriend to care-take the neighboring ranch. Maria fed the men a hearty breakfast. She and Mr. Garcia often sat close together on the porch where they murmured and giggled privately. There was clearly something brewing there. The children came every day with Maria, and I could hear their joyful shrieks as they played in the pool.

The only person out of place was Paul.

I said tactfully, "Have you thought about when you're going back to New York?"

He said "No, why?"

He insisted he wanted to help. And he did try. He would occasionally pull up a plant and bring it to me to identify it as a weed or not, or he would pour some water on a cactus.

But mostly he was bored, languishing with his feet up on the porch rail, drinking coffee. One day when Mr. Garcia's men were about to wrap up for the day, Paul ambled over to the big yellow grader. He climbed up and started messing with the controls, and somehow got the engine in gear. It seemed like a triumphant moment to him, and he whooped loudly, but then the rig started to roll. Paul seemed to be unable to find the brake.

The big machine lumbered down the drive in a direct line for the stable where Appie lived.

Luckily Francisco was in there grooming him. He heard the rumble growing louder and shot out of the stable and ran across the dirt and clambered up on board the yellow rig. He wrenched the wheel hard, swinging the tractor off its deadly course. The sharp turn caused Paul to be tossed out of the cab and thrown to the ground.

Paul moaned about his bruises, blaming Francisco for his injuries, but nobody was listening. Paul's whining was drowned out by the praise Francisco received for having saved the horse. A photographer came and took photos for the local paper. Appie posed nicely, that horse sure knows a camera, and Francisco stood smiling next to him. The front-page story gave my fledgling business a strong boost of publicity. As did the wedding of Maria and Mr. Garcia. That was in the paper too. The children of course, were ecstatic, running around like wild things.

Somewhere in all of this, Paul was forgotten. I didn't even see him go. I suppose he and his purple jacket are now enjoying the opera in New York.

ALL OUR ANGELS

The Nazi outpost was just up the road. The soldiers occasionally marched in formation through the village on patrol, largely for show, and largely ignored by the villagers. The villagers were preoccupied by the daily effort to survive.

My grandfather had given in to despair. He went out into the field one day and shot a rabbit for our dinner, and then turned his gun on himself. He was buried in the village cemetery. He left behind a bitter and unforgiving widow, who was angry that he would abandon her to struggle alone, having already lost her son to the war, and now having to provide for an orphaned grandchild.

I was that child. She made sure that I worked for my keep. I rose before dawn each day to light the stove, and to carry in water from the outside pump. I laundered our clothes in the old tin tub, my fingers raw from the splintered washboard. I scavenged in the stripped forest for twigs to burn for cooking, and I worked in the vegetable garden, weeding, and hoeing until my arms and back ached and it was too dark to see. I scrubbed our floor and shook out the thread-bare mats. My grandmother observed my handiwork with a critical eye, her deeply lined face closed and grim. But I did notice that when there was very little food for us to eat, she put it all on my plate, and claimed she wasn't hungry.

I rose even earlier on market day to cut the cabbages. We had our seasonal vegetables to barter for what we needed. I trudged behind her along the dusty road, the full sack bending my back and scratching me through my thin dress. My broken shoes cut into my feet as I tried to keep up.

Some villagers were already there, setting up their wares around the edges of the village square. We were about to settle into our usual spot under a tree when we heard it, the unmistakable stuttering putt-putt of an airplane in distress. And then we saw it spiraling downward, a slab-sided B-24 Liberator, feathered plume trailing as it nosedived into a nearby field. There was silence, all eyes turned skyward, looking to the heavens, waiting. Suddenly, the stark outline of a figure came into view. A cry went up as it floated out of the clouds, like an angel on white parachute wings.

Dropping my sack, I pushed my way through the crowd in time to see the American land in the middle of the village square. Everyone watched in silence as the young man disentangled himself and crawled clear of his white shroud. Oily smudges streaked his apple cheeks, his uniform was tattered, and blood oozed from a gash in one arm. He staggered to his feet and looked about him. Surrounded by staring villagers, there was no point in trying to run. So he straightened, and standing at attention, he turned to face the rows of gaping people.

The growl of an engine grew louder. Churning up dirt and stones, its side car rattling noisily, the motorcycle pulled to the edge of the square. The German soldier's high boot caught in the footrest as he dismounted, and he stumbled, and his helmet fell off. His blond hair flopped as he ran forward, awkwardly tugging at his leather holster. The crowd parted so that he had a clear view of the stranger. The German soldier took tentative steps forward, still grappling with the flap that secured his Luger. The young American pulled a white handkerchief from his pocket and dropped to his knees. The white cloth fluttered in the breeze as he held it up high. The German finally freed his revolver, and pointed it at the American, and for a long moment the two stared at each other. They could have been two young football players staring at the rival team.

A sudden thunderous blast rent the air, jolting everyone, as the downed plane exploded. The startled villagers turned toward the flames and the black smoke rising over the hedgerows. Then they turned back to the square. The young American looked bewildered, his eyes uncomprehending, his mouth forming a round O of surprise, and then, still holding the white handkerchief up high, he slowly crumpled to the ground.

The German soldier was transfixed with shock, his face ashen, his arm still outstretched, the hand that held the smoldering gun wobbled uncontrollably. He glanced nervously at the crowd, uncertain what to do next. He looked over his shoulder as though expecting a battalion of his comrades to come roaring down the road to rescue him. The crowd began to mutter, and the soldier whirled, and pointed his gun at them.

The crowd shrank back.

Suddenly my grandmother burst through the wall of people. She ran across the square. The German soldier spun around, focusing his gun on her.

He shrieked, "Halt!" His eyes were wild as he took a crouch position and brought his other hand up to steady the gun, his aim following the racing woman. A collective gasp went up from the crowd.

"Halt!" he screamed again.

My grandmother's step didn't falter. Her rough boots clattered on the cobbles as she ran. She dropped to her knees beside the young American, and tenderly raised his head to her breast. She held him close to her, as gently as if he were her own child. She murmured to him and rocked him, and he died there on the hard stones, in a foreign place far from home.

ALL THAT GLITTERS ISN'T GOLD

The wife is looking disapprovingly at my short skirt. I know when the wife is there you should never pay attention to the husband, but because of the way he looks right through her, and more importantly, because I checked the title and there's only one name on it and it's not hers, I know I can ignore her.

A lot has happened very fast. I am the newest, the youngest, and greenest realtor in the company. I looked around at our weekly meeting, a few men but mostly women with 20 years of experience on me, all a bit jaded, weary of dicey clients. But I know I am going to be good at this. I sailed through every question and the Proctor looked up in surprise when I handed in my license exam paper early and left.

At the company meetings I dream of the day when I can take the podium to announce my first listing. I am proud to be one of them. All of us look very impressive as a group, a wall of company gold. We look good from a distance when we have our business image on, but our yellow jackets aren't very good quality. I had to take a needle and thread to reinforce my buttons, and I know the other realtors complain about fraying hems. The company motto is honesty rah rah, and the public eats that up, we are the most successful brokerage in town, with not a whiff of scandal. But our agents lock their desks at night. I heard that our broker has more than once stolen someone else's client with offers of greater experience, contacts, and bargaining power.

I was sitting Floor. It's where beginners start. Seasoned realtors avoid Floor Time. They develop contacts through clubs and referrals. Newbies like me have no other way to get clients, other than door-knocking. I tried that once.

"Hi, I'm a real estate agent and I was just in the neighborhood …" It was tedious, tiring, and time-consuming. Lonely people tell you their life story, busy people are just this side of rude. Though Floor Time isn't much better. If there are ten calls in an afternoon, nine will be vendors trying to sell us their services, and one will be a New Yorker, looking to make a killing.

"Is there anything under $500 thousand?" they'll say.

"Nope, never has been, never will be."

"Well, is there anyone under water …?"

"You mean desperate, losing their shirt, house foreclosing? Nope. But there is a small, converted garage studio next to the railroad tracks for one mill five." Click.

The call came in around noon, just as I was about to pack up. The man asked for Phyllis, he said that he knows somebody who maybe knows her from tennis. Phyllis was in the restroom, so I said, in my prettiest voice, that she's not in, but I would be happy to help. The man said he wants to sell and gave an address. We made an appointment.

I want him to think I am successful, so I wear all my gold jewelry. It is gold plated stuff, not real, just graduation and 21st birthday gifts, some clanking bangles, dangling earrings and a gold chain necklace. I add a couple of flashy rings and a spritz of Jovan Musk on my wrists. I did get my nails done. People have complimented me on my hands, so I want to be sure he notices them. I had the girl add a little glitter, muted, nothing too outrageous.

I leave my car a block away. I don't have the de rigueur silver 450 SL. Yet. I walk up the driveway to a very big house in the prestigious Torley Hill section of Wellport. He meets me at the door. I am surprised to see a woman standing behind him. He hadn't mentioned a wife. She's got bleached Lauren Bacall hair and she's wearing a designer muumuu that hides whatever's wrong with her figure.

"We're moving to Lake Como, Italy," she brags.

She has vertical smokers' wrinkles on her upper lip, and a raspy drinker's voice. I don't answer or look at her. I let the dead air linger, to show that her salvo has missed its mark. I lay my business card on the foyer table. I don't risk trying to hand it to her, she might not take it and then I would lose that round. Mr. G is watching us, his hands clasped behind his back, uninvolved, but his little deep-set black eyes are darting from one to the other, amused.

"Here's our listings," I say, laying the stack next to my card. None of them are mine, of course, but I am hoping that he doesn't know that. "Would you like to show me around?" I say it to nobody in particular, I'm waiting to see who's the power partner. The wife steps forward, a little too quickly, she's trying too hard.

As Mr. G and I walk behind her, it's clear that it's his house. He had said on the phone, "Call me Mr. G," implying that his name is something unpronounceable. His taste is likewise incomprehensible. The house is crammed with ornate imported furniture, gold chandeliers, gilt framed mirrors, over-stuffed crimson chairs, velvet gold-tasseled curtains, huge glass-front curio cabinets, and carpets so thick you have to step up so as not to trip. It's over-decorated and over-embellished, especially for a beach town, even a celebrity-laden town like Wellport. It's not American taste, it's even miles beyond garish new money American taste.

The wife is walking, talking. "This is the kitchen."

"Really?" I murmur, as though that is a revelation. Mr. G and I exchange involuntary smirks. I let her talk, she's digging herself into a hole, she misunderstands her position here. At the maid's bedroom, Mr. G has had enough. He turns and walks away. I quickly follow him, leaving the wife standing alone gesturing at window treatments.

She's now so far down the leader board, I can be nice to her.

"Where would you like me to sit," I say to her, but I am already arranging my clipboard, pens, and the listing documents on Mr. G's desk, and settling in across from him.

The wife has no choice but to take a chair on the other side of the room. She lights a cigarette.

"I think perhaps we should use a more experienced realtor ..." she says, and pauses.

The only sound is a ticking clock.

Mr. G pulls out a monogrammed pen and holds it ready. I am so green, it takes me a second. I thought I would have to haggle over list price and commission, sell him on my services, all the things we've been taught to do back at the office. I slide the documents over to him, and he starts signing.

He's obviously sold a ton of property; he doesn't read the boilerplate and barely glances at the rest. We haven't discussed list price, and I don't dare lean forward to see what he has written. I don't want to insult him by watching him sign, that would insinuate that I don't trust him, so I sit back and rearrange the papers on my clipboard.

I am enjoying the sense of camaraderie of us two business professionals working together cozily at his desk, while she, the wife, is over there, left out.

When he pushes the paperwork back to me, I just want to get out of there. I am giddy with excitement as I shove everything in my briefcase. The wife is blowing smoke rings. I want her to stay there in her chair, I want Mr. G to walk me out, so I go over to her and I say elaborate thank-yous and goodbyes. She looks up at me. I expect to see defeat in her eyes. What I see sends a jolt into my gut. The look is perceptive, shrewd, knowing. Just a flash. She stays in her chair.

Mr. G walks me across the wide foyer, I'm chattering brightly about nothing. At the door, I touch Mr. G's arm, just a light touch on the forearm, perhaps a bit too intimate for a business situation, but my palms are damp so I can't do a professional handshake. The smell of his cologne hangs in my nostrils.

I say to him, wagging my finger playfully, "Now Mr. G, it's always better if the owner isn't at the open house, OK?"

"Yes, yes," he laughs and throws up his hands. "I know, I know. I'll be good."

I make myself walk slowly and calmly down the driveway. I swing my hips a little so that my short skirt swishes from side to side. I don't hear the front door closing, so I know he is watching.

Back at the office, I pull out the listing. The broker has to sign it. She's flabbergasted that I have it, but then she points out blank signature blocks.

"It's not legal," she says. "I can't sign off on it. Do you want me to help you?"

I grab the paperwork off her desk, she's not getting anywhere near my client, I've heard the rumors. I tell her I'll get it fixed.

The day of my first open house. My gold jacket has been freshened at the dry cleaners, and I'm wearing my trade-mark short black skirt and my highest heels. I open the double front doors wide, ready for my visitors, and I go upstairs. I am busy pulling back all the heavy drapes, bringing light into the fusty rooms, when I hear a car door slam. My heart leaps, my first visitor, they are early so they must be really interested in buying. I was going to run downstairs to greet them, but I am too eager to see what they look like. I peep out the window, craning to see the driveway, trying to get a glimpse.

It's him. It's Mr. G, and he's alone. He picks up my open-house sign and carries it with him into the house. I hear both the front doors slam shut in unison, and the heavy iron lock thuds into place. And then I hear his footsteps on the stairs.

IT'S ALL ABOUT THE CHINA

Dear Mum,

Hope you are well. Yesterday we explored the inside of the Great Pyramid. It's called the Khufu Pyramid, it's a monument to Khufu, aka Cheops, an ancient Egyptian monarch with a somewhat murky reputation. It is the biggest of the three pyramids that make up one of the Seven Wonders of the Ancient World. Only a limited number of people are allowed inside daily, but one of the Egyptologists on our archaeology team offered to give us a private tour. I love studying the languages, culture and history of ancient Egypt. Looking back, I realize how very lucky I was to get accepted. There were hundreds of applicants from all around England, so I am really thrilled that Oxford chose me. This is a photo of my team. That's me in the middle. I have a great tan now from the sun. Love to Junie and the children, Pat

Pat.

I got your letter. I was opening it when Mrs. Shankle, you know, the woman who lives next door, was hanging over the fence and your photo fell out. She looked at it and said who are all those men standing around in back of her. I said it doesn't matter, none of them will marry her because her skin is all wrinkled from the sun. Junie is well, but she is uncomfortable from her pregnancy. Mum

Dear Mum,

This is a very intensive course. We are just a small group, but I am able to develop my archeology skills working with Egyptian artefacts in the collections at the museum. We are off to the fabulous city of Luxor tomorrow; it's got amazing temples on both sides of the Nile. We are going to start our fieldwork soon; we will be digging at the Abusir site. I am looking forward to working there, it's a brand-new dig just discovered. Love to Junie and the children. Pat

Pat.
The woman next door, you know, Mrs. Shankle, asked me what you're doing wherever you are. I said you were digging up rocks. Anyway, the lady from Services came round. She was very serious, she told me they may have to take away the children because a member of our family is in jail. I said what do you mean in jail. She said well it's all around the neighborhood that my other daughter is on a chain gang somewhere. I suppose Mrs. Shankle next door spread that. Look at the trouble you are causing for the family. Junie is very uncomfortable with her back and her swollen ankles. Mum

Dear Mum,
I just had to share the good news with you. We have found ancient burial shafts at Abusir, we think they belong to the elite Egyptian society that lived here during the 26th Dynasty. That was 664 to 525 BC. Can you imagine! We are over the moon because it seems to have been a mummification workshop! What could be more exciting! Our whole team is going to be working on the project together, I am so excited to be working with such knowledgeable people. Who knows what antiquities we will find. I have to run, we need to be there at the crack of dawn. Love to Junie and the children. Pat

Pat.
Junie brought her beau to tea the other day. He is a very big fella. Mrs. Shankle next door was hanging over the fence gawking. Anyway, he came in. He's got a funny accent. Well, you know me, I am not backward in coming forward. So I said since our Junie is showing, shall we expect a wedding soon. He said no, he has a wife back in Africa, and he has been trying to bring her here. He must not like English food, he just took one sip of his tea, and he left all his cake, and he bolted out the door. They're a funny lot, everyone says so. Mum

Dear Mum,
Well, our excavation is becoming world famous. The site is giving up all kinds of treasures. We have found hundreds of artefacts, including gorgeous ancient Egyptian vases used for storing oil, water, and wine. They are amphora-shaped pots, some of them even still have mummification residue of resin and myrrh! Can you imagine, from so long ago? I am busy writing my dissertation, and I have been invited to make a presentation at the museum on Friday! Break a leg and fingers crossed it goes well, right? Love to Junie and the children. Pat

Pat.
I looked in the boxes you had stored here. There were just some old books with pictures of broken china, so I threw them out. Mrs. Shankle was looking over the fence. She said a girl with hoity-toity degrees won't ever get a man. Well, she got me there, there was nothing I could say to that. The dustbin was full up, and the garbage men were pissed off.

You really shouldn't leave all your old rubbish lying around. We need the room for the children's toys. Some of your dresses were hanging there as well. Junie can't wear them, she has a much more womanly figure than you, so she cut them down to fit her girls Veronica and Charlene, and she made a sweet romper for little Susie and bibs for Mikey. Unfortunately, there was nothing young Teddy could wear. The house next door on the other side of us from Mrs. Shankle is still for sale. A nice older couple came to see it. They looked over the fence and said who do all these children belong to, do you run a nursery school here? I said no they are my grandchildren, and there's another one on the way. They didn't buy the house. Mum

Dear Mum,

It's hard to believe that even this small dig, it's only about two square kilometers, has so much to tell us. We've so far only dug about two percent of it, but we've already found so many artefacts of cultural and historical interest. We are examining the extraordinary and previously unheard-of accomplishments of ancient people, and how they may affect the future of all humankind. And big news, I have been offered a docent position at the museum, starting when I get my doctoral degree in archaeology! They thanked me for all my hard work. I couldn't believe my good luck. And I've got a big surprise for you, after three years of working here I am being given a short holiday! I will be coming home to see you! I don't suppose you could let Dad know? Love to Junie and the children. Pat

Pat.

Don't you be asking me about your Dad. I've been ever so lonely since your Dad left. If you had been a boy, your Dad maybe wouldn't have left. Since we already had a girl, we were ever so disappointed. We had already picked out a boy's name, Patrick, and then you popped out. I named you Pat, I thought your Dad could pretend. But he left anyway. The house next door is still for sale. It has been for ages. People come and look over the fence and congratulate me on all my lovely grandchildren, but none of them have bought the house. It's about time you came home to help Junie with the children, it's not fair she has to do it all alone. Well, you always were the selfish one. Young Veronica, you know, Junie's oldest, is looking forward to seeing her Auntie Pat. She asked if you were coming to dinner and I said yes, and she said could we use the best china. I said no Love, that's only for special occasions. We'll save it for when Junie has her baby. Mum

FEET OF CLAY

The sky to the west was dusted with breathtaking streaks of pink and purple as I set out. I jogged down the road, pleased I could just get in a quick loop through the park to finish my day.

"I can just squeeze this in, last thing to check off on my To Do list, and I'll be back in time for the News," I murmured to myself. I talk out loud to keep myself company on runs.

I had just turned in at the park gate when I realized I had left the house in such a hurry I had left my cell phone on the counter. But I had at least slipped my ID into my sock. Right then I was very tempted to just turn around and go back the way I had come, along the busy road.

But, and I said it out loud, "That's b-o-r-i-n-g," and I let momentum carry me on to the well-marked park trail. I waved to a woman running in the opposite direction. We made eye contact, both of us smiled, a momentary bond of companionship. Seeing another woman running there at dusk reinforced my decision to keep going. Rationally I was aware that she was now near the gate about to exit the park while I was beginning a run through the park, but I ignored that because I wanted to keep going.

The trail dipped down into a valley, and I took childish pleasure in skipping from stone to stone across the swirling brook.

"Making good time. This girl's crushing it."

But that was the end of the downhill stretch. The terrain changed, the path became rocky, and angled steeply upward. I tried to keep a steady pace, and though I felt myself flagging, I denied myself a rest break. I kept going to beat the fading light, now partially hidden behind the leafy canopy. My feet became heavier, and I had to fight rising uneasiness as the light continued to wane and dark trunks and thick brush seemed to close in on me.

The trail eventually flattened out and wood chips replaced the rocks. In the distance I spotted limestone pillars, pearly grey in the gloom, and beyond the gates, car headlights streaming along the busy road.

I tried to pick up my pace. "Hup, hup, hup," I encouraged myself. "Surely I've got another gear in here."

Relieved that in a few minutes I'd be back into civilization, I willed my legs to push through each stride. I focused on my goal, my quick rasping breaths drowning out any other sound.

"Almost there, almost …"

The corner of my eye caught the tip of a blue sneaker moving up alongside, and simultaneously I felt a sharp blow, and my head exploded, and I was falling, helplessly dropping through space. And then, oblivion.

I awoke to complete and total blackness.

My eyes strained to see. "Am I blind?" I wondered, "Why don't my eyes work?"

My jacket was wet, and my body was chilled and stiff, and ached as though I had been lying in one position for hours. The pungent odor of rotted leaves filled my nostrils. Twigs crackled, and something wet, cold and bristly nuzzled my cheek. I recoiled, my mouth open to scream, but no sound came out. Then the dog barked, and a bobbing light pierced the dark.

"Are you OK?"

Relief rushed like a hot river through my veins. I bit back a sharp retort, does it really look like I'm OK, lying here flat on my back and buried in compost in the middle of the night? In a sudden flash of panic, I checked my jeans, but they were still zipped, buttoned and intact.

"Yeah, I'm fine. Oh boy, am I glad to see you! I think a branch fell on my head." My attempt at a flippant laugh came out as a croak.

"Here let me help you, can you stand up?"

"Yes, I think so."

He put his flashlight between his teeth and pulled me to my feet. The dog snuffled at my legs, trying to help.

"My car is right at the park entrance," the man said. "Can I give you a ride home?"

"Yes, yes, please. I really think I am done jogging for now."

My head was heavy, the world spun. I lurched forward. He encircled my body with a muscular arm. My legs made walking motions, but I don't think either of my feet connected with the ground. He half carried and half dragged me the short distance to his car. The road was now deserted, no-one had anywhere to go at this hour. I was grateful for my good luck in being found.

I sank into the soft leather, and let the seat cradle me. The dog flopped down behind me, his doggy smell filling the car.

"Address?"

I pulled my ID from my sock and gave it to him and lulled by the warmth of the heater and muted strains from the radio, I closed my eyes.

When the purr of the engine and the gentle rocking ceased, I realized we were in front of my house. The man cut the lights and ran around to my side and motioned me to get out. I obediently dangled my feet where I thought the ground should be. He had to catch me.

I heard him say, "Stay Hunter, I'll be right back."

"People will think you are bringing home a drunk," I said to hide my embarrassment. He heaved me up onto the porch. I fumbled for my keys, my fingers unwieldy as cabbages, and I struggled to stay upright. He took the keys out of my hand, and opened the door, and moved me inside.

"Where do you want me to put you? How about the couch? Is the couch OK?"

"Yes, yes. Thank you so much." My aching head sank into a soft cushion, and I let out an audible sigh that my ordeal was over. I had got through it without harm, I could cross a run off my To Do list, and I was safe and sound back at home.

I heard his footsteps return to the door.

"Thank you!" I called.

The door closed, and at the click of the latch, I opened my eyes. I wondered foggily why I could still see him standing there. And that's when I saw his blue tennis shoes.

THE SOLITARY CHILD

She remembered the cavernous station, the hulking black steam locomotives on every track waiting to swallow up the children. Like champion racehorses they restlessly snorted, their choking steam and clanking, grating machinery only added to the air of frantic urgency to move before the bombs came. The engineers steadily shoveled coke, their faces glowing red from the fires as they fed each gaping maw. Mothers and fathers held back tears, lips quivering as they exhorted their children to be brave, even when they themselves were not.

One child seemed apart from the others. She stood there on the platform with her small suitcase, the white destination tag secured by a cord around her neck. She had no-one with her, and with no emotional good-byes to delay her, she climbed up the iron steps and obediently took her seat where she was told. The whistle blew, and as the train jerked forward and chuffed out of the station, the other children leaned out of the windows, their tags swinging as the train gathered speed, waving until the platform slid out of view. The solitary child was already curled up in a corner, asleep.

For many hours through the night, the train steamed north. The child slept deeply, oblivious to any stops. A woman eventually came and gently shook her awake and pulled her little suitcase from the overhead rack. The uniformed station master blew his whistle and raised his arm, and the big black train strained and heaved, and moved forward, leaving the child on the gravel platform.

The child gazed at the green fields stretching to the horizon, her stomach knotted with misery. The sign on one of the whitewashed stone buildings said *Craigallechie*. And in case a traveler had somehow forgotten where he was going, a hand-written notice tacked to the wall added helpfully, *Aberlour to Dufftown via Craigellachie*. Tall signal poles stood at attention next to the tracks, and an iron walkway arched above, connecting the two platforms. The child's eyes hungrily scanned the route to the platform returning south.

Someone behind her coughed. Two people stood smiling at her. One took her suitcase, and each took a hand, and she walked between them to the village. They spoke in muted tones in a language she did not understand.

"…. is tae auld. Howfur kin she care fur a wee bairn. She cannae tak' care o' a wee bairn."

The child knew she was the "wee bairn" because of the ever-so-slight inclination of their heads in her direction.

Miss Dunbar met them at her door. Tall and sinewy, she appeared as fragile as a dried twig. Boney ankles peeped beneath the hem of her long dress, and her black laced up shoes creaked. Her face was deeply lined, but remarkable for the kind eyes, crinkling at the corners in welcome. The faint scent of lavender wafted behind her as she led the child into the house.

Miss Dunbar had tatted the edge of a white hankie, and she handed it to the child as a gift. Then she heaved a cauldron of hot water from its peg over the fire and filled a tin bathtub. The child looked about her. There was no mirrored sideboard with fine painted china, her feet did not sink into deep patterned carpets, there were no plush upholstered chairs, no tinkling glass chandeliers. The toilet was a shed in the garden next to a coop, and now this, a tin bathtub in front of the kitchen fire. Miss Dunbar mistook the child's hesitation for modesty and hobbled out to tend to her chickens.

The child could find the school easily in that tiny village. Miss Dunbar was too frail to walk with her, of course. The classroom was bare, simple, and Miss Fiona's large wooden desk was on a raised platform. When the bell rang for recess, the other children ran out, chattering and laughing together. The child didn't understand their speech and saw no reason to join them. She hung behind at her desk, pretending to read a book full of the foreign words. Miss Fiona also stayed in the classroom, feet up, her swollen belly straining at her print dress, busily knitting for the baby.

Noticing the child, she waved an apple as enticement, and said, "Bade wi' me, we wull slock th'gither." She used her foot to push her stool toward the child. She knew English and was pleased to practice it. "Dinnae slock the seeds, dinnae eat the seeds," she cautioned, as she carefully cut out the apple core. She made a grotesque face, with bulging eyes and protruding tongue, gasping for air to mimic being poisoned by the seeds. Miss Fiona laughed merrily, but the child did not laugh, she was already beginning to form a plan.

The rhythmic click of Miss Fiona's needles kept time with her gay chatter. The sun streamed in and lit the wisps of blond hair crowning her head like the Madonna's halo. Miss Fiona delighted in this child who preferred to keep her company rather than go out and play. The child watched when the core, the part with the apple seeds, was thrown into the waste bucket. She ate slowly, making her apple slice last. When Miss Fiona put down her knitting and hurried down the hall to the toilets, as pregnant woman must do frequently, the child collected the seeds from the bucket and hid them in her shoe.

She found a stone in the schoolyard and brought it home. That night, she crushed the apple pits and wrapped them in her embroidered hankie. She did not feel Miss Dunbar's kind hands tucking the rough hand-sewn quilt around her. She could only long for her own comfortable feather eiderdown and soft white sheets. She listened to the owl that went whoo whoo whoo in the night, just like the train whistle had as it pulled away from the station, the train that would come back and carry her home to London.

Each morning the breakfast ritual was the same. Miss Dunbar would put out two bowls of hot porridge, one for herself and one for the child, and lovingly add a pinch of sugar to the child's bowl. When steam would hiss and shoot from the kettle spout, and the lid would lift and dance excitedly, Miss Dunbar would get up from the table, swirl some hot water in the teapot, put in exactly two level scoops of tea leaves from the painted tin, and then pour in boiling water. The making of the tea took several minutes.

The child waited her chance, and reached into her pocket and untwisted the hankie, and took some of the crushed apple pits, and sprinkled them into Miss Dunbar's porridge. She gave it a quick stir, careful to replace the spoon to exactly the same position. Miss Dunbar would finish her porridge with dainty bites. The child watched and waited, expecting at any moment Miss Dunbar would clutch at her throat, make loud gasping noises, and fall to the floor. But instead, each morning Miss Dunbar would finish her porridge, and with both elbows resting on the table, hands warming around the cup, she would savor her morning tea.

Four months later, Miss Fiona told the child that the English government had reversed the evacuation and she could go home. Miss Dunbar came to the door to say goodbye, but the child raced to Miss Fiona's side without a backward glance. She was impatient that Miss Fiona's bulk caused her to walk so slowly. They climbed the steps to the iron bridge and crossed to the southbound platform, as the child had dreamed of for so long. When the train came, Miss Fiona flung her arms around the child, and too choked to speak, she touched her lips to the child's forehead. But the child pushed her aside and eagerly climbed up into the train.

The concrete canyons blocked the light and seemed to close in on the people swarming about, pushing and shoving, mindlessly jostling each other. A cacophony of blaring horns screamed from all sides. The soot-filled air caught in the child's throat as the driver delivered her like a parcel to the door. A housekeeper she had never seen before let her in and took her coat. Her father was away on business it seemed, and her mother busy elsewhere.

Not many months later, a letter in a familiar hand arrived for her. Miss Fiona was writing to say that Miss Dunbar had gone peacefully to be with the angels, and how Miss Dunbar had spoken of the child often and remembered her fondly.

ESCAPE 1

The pit bull hurtled toward me, teeth bared, snarling. I was trying to get out of my front door to go to work, but the dog was right there, barring my way. I jangled my keys at it, but it snapped at me ferociously, asserting its newly won territory on my front step. I shouted to his owner, my neighbor. I could see her, she was in her front yard, chattering on her cellphone, gesturing animatedly.

I reached for the garden broom and brandished the handle end at the dog. I didn't want to get his slobber on the bristles. The dog leapt up and savagely clamped its jaws on the pointy end. I tried to pull it out of his mouth, but in an unanticipated and poorly thought-out move, the dog lunged forward, and succeeded only in shoving the handle down his own throat. Gagging, his jaws reflexively flew open, and the broom clattered to the ground. The dog scrambled over the fence and ran up the road.

I got in my car and headed for work. I saw the dog running ahead of me, staggering drunkenly from side to side, shaking his head, spittle flying, trying to remove what was no longer in his throat. He was blindly heading for the highway.

The first car hit him broadside and flung him into the opposite lane. A north bound U-Haul clipped him on the downward arc, and the wheels of a garbage truck following behind rolled right over him. I could hear his bones crunching as I headed south, leaving the scene of my first murder.

ESCAPE 2

T he man watched a barge head upstream in the inky waters. A buoy's clanking stridently broke through the dense fog. The sweet stench of rotting weeds filled his nostrils, swords of canary grass pierced his thin clothing. His ears strained for any unusual sound over the chorus of insects and ceaselessly gurgling of the river. The damp seeped into his bones, and he longed to stretch and relieve the ache in his limbs, and rub the ankle that held the broken chain, but he was fearful any movement might give away his hiding place. He felt his head droop but forced his eyes open to continue their vigilance.

A lamp flickered briefly in the distance, the sound of voices grew, and then faded.

Stick to the river, they had told him, the river will show you the way. He had come this far, and there was no going back. He took comfort in the moonless night which gave him cover to rest, but terror would come with the dawn. He knew he would have to get up and run, but not whether his exhausted limbs would be able to carry him. Like a burrowing animal he dug deeper into the mud and waited for the light.

He was jerked awake by a snorting growl in his own throat, and he realized that sleep had claimed him, and sleep had betrayed him. He opened his eyes, blinking in the harsh yellow glare of a lantern. A slender gangling youth, hardly out of childhood, fishing pole in hand, stood looking down at him from the bank, his face a mask of shock and surprise. For a long moment man and boy gazed at each other, then the boy vanished, and the man was alone.

On the opposite bank, amber threads of light crept over the dark tree line. A barge's deep resonant blast sounded in the distance; the rhythmic chugging of its motor hung on the still air. Water licked at the man's feet. And the man knew what he had to do.

He slid across the mud and was swallowed by the water's cool embrace. He swam out to the middle of the river. There, he rolled onto his back and drifted, floating, watching as the lighted wheelhouse grew larger. Then, at just the right moment, he turned over onto his belly, and fighting the backwash, he swam with resolute strokes until he was alongside the barge.

In the new morning light, his eyes scanned its wooden sides for any dangling rope he could grasp, anything he could cling to. His fingers curled around a line, and like a child at its mother's breast, he hung on, willing himself to be carried far from this place.

THE PLAYER

Joseph grasped the pommel and struggled to understand why he was even sitting on a horse. The pommel was his only hope of staying in the saddle. His eyes didn't focus, and his head felt as though it was floating away from his body.

From somewhere in the deep recesses of his fog, the often-practiced line rose to the surface, and he mumbled his seven words, slid sideways, and fell to the ground. It was a fluid and graceful fall. The Director yelled "Cut!" visibly relieved they finally got the take. He applauded, and the cast and crew dutifully followed suit. The sound of a rifle shot would be dubbed in later.

Joseph didn't move, so a crew member ran over to help him up, they needed the area to prepare the next scene before the light faded. When he couldn't be roused, the crew carried Joseph out of camera range, and EMTs were called. Try though they might, there was nothing the professionals could do to help Joseph, and he was tagged and bagged and taken away. The Director thought it would look insensitive if the media broadcast the story first, so he asked a gaffer who was idle and between scenes, to go and tell Margaret that Joseph had died.

Joseph and Margaret lived in a tiny rundown North Hollywood apartment. At the end of their first year together there, Joseph had suggested to Margaret that they go out to dinner to celebrate. Margaret was thrilled and headed for an uptown boutique. The dress was two sizes too small, and the saleswoman tried to keep a straight face as she tugged at the zipper trying to close it. Margaret was proud of the way her breasts bulged over the top of the dress. They were really expensive, even in Tijuana. She was saving for lip fillers next, but she was hesitant after she read that a movie star had been disfigured by an injection of low-grade motor oil from some charlatan in Argentina.

Margaret had begun her self-improvement project to impress Joseph. Joseph pretended she did this body work for herself, out of vanity. He had taken for granted her doting admiration of him all through and ever since their small-town high school days. He wounded her daily with remarks about her cellulite, her bulging midriff, the rasping noise her thighs made when she walked. Margaret tried every diet, Palo, Keto, vegan, 16-hour fasts, Atkins, Weight Watchers. Margaret skipped meals and for days drank nothing but lemon juice laced with cayenne pepper, until she started dry retching. The Hollywood Curves gym asked her to leave when she became so dizzy she fell off the treadmill, but she suspected it was really because her size was a bad image for their brand. Her mother had told her all the women in the family were big-boned, and to marry a farmer.

Margaret bought trendy fashionable clothes at online sales, but Joseph was not happy with that either. He complained she was frittering away all their money. "Their" money in reality was her money, he never acknowledged that she waitressed to support his dream.

When she came back to their cramped little studio apartment each day, her feet and back ached dreadfully, and she noticed in the mirror that the all-day compulsory smiling at customers was adding lines to her face. She always sneaked a small tiramisu out of the restaurant for Joseph, she knew he loved those. Other than gobbling down the dessert, he didn't pay any attention to her, instead focusing on his acting career.

She was very lonely in the evenings, sitting in an uncomfortable Ikea accent chair, thumbing through movie magazines while he practiced acting. Sometimes she even thought of giving up and going home. Everyone had warned her, the town pretty-boy is not a keeper. But she was too embarrassed to face the mean girls back home. She knew Joseph eyed the models and starlets hungrily, knowing that if only one of *them* was on his arm, his career could start to soar. Meanwhile he made do with Margaret.

So, he had invited her to a posh dinner in a real restaurant. Margaret tucked the price tag into her bra, planning on returning the dress to the shop the next day, and chattered brightly to Joseph throughout the meal, trying to be good company. Exactly an hour later, she was mid-sentence when Joseph suddenly stood up, and told her it was time to leave. Margaret took the tiny steps the dress allowed, trying to keep up with Joseph as he hurried to the door.

The photographers had shown up at precisely the time Joseph's anonymous phone call told them to, and Joseph quickly got into position, with a surprised, "Oh ha ha, you guys are absolutely everywhere!"

He stood framed in the restaurant doorway, angled slightly, looking over one shoulder with a seductive half smile. He had seen a photo of Tab Hunter doing that once, and he had practiced it.

The photographers suddenly stopped clicking and stared. They had noticed Margaret as she came into view with her very eye-catching décolletage, and they moved in to get a much more interesting shot.

Joseph quickly stepped in front of her.

"Lovely dinner, celebrating my first year in Hollywood!" he called out, even though no-one had asked.

Margaret murdered Joseph on a Friday. Not all at once of course, but bit by bit, for months drizzling sweet drops of anti-freeze into his tiramisu. She knew it had been on a Friday because that was the day FedEx delivered her package.

She had eagerly ripped open the tough plastic and whipped out the double-breasted red blazer and tried it on. It didn't fit, and the padded shoulders made her look like a linebacker. Tears of disappointment ran down her cheeks.

When the gaffer knocked on her door to tell her Joseph had died, he saw her tears and said, "Oh, you already know. Nice jacket."

THE DINGO FENCE

Thehere's nothing out here. I wanted to go to Cancun and lie next to the pool and drink for two weeks. All my buddies went to Cancun. But oh no, *you* had to have us come to some fucking … I mean it's 110, even with the A/C it's 80 in here. And what's even to see?" He stared moodily out the car window. "It's all a big empty nothing."

"I thought it would be interesting. Besides, you had three years of your buddies, aren't you just a little sick of them by now?"

"They are my best friends I'll have you know. Where are *your* friends, do you even *have* any friends?"

"No, I was too busy working."

Eugene gave an exasperated tsk. "Oh, Angela, don't even. Just don't even go there again."

"Well, it's the truth. I made it possible for you."

"Yeah, right, like there was nothing in it for you. It was as much for you, you know, you wanted the status of being a lawyer's wife."

"That's not true, and you know it."

"And you had to prove to your parents you didn't marry a loser."

"What? They never said that."

"Yeah, but they thought it. I noticed how your Dad looked at me."

The silence was heavy. After a long spell, he turned toward her, grinning. He leaned over and tickled her neck.

"Wanna fuck?"

"No."

"Aw, come on, nobody's gonna see us out here."

"No."

He leaned over and tried to nibble on her earlobe. She raised her shoulder to ward him off. He threw himself back in his seat.

After a long time, he said. "I'm sorry, I'm sorry, I'm sorry, OK? There, you happy? I said I'm sorry."

"Yes, but you don't mean it."

"Look, I get it. You had to do three years of 9 to 5 for an asshole. I get it. But I had to study hard to get through. It wasn't all on you. It wasn't easy for me either, you know."

He looked at her for a long moment. Her face was set and closed. She was looking down at her hands, twisting the edge of the map. The only sound was the whoosh of the air conditioning. He suddenly jerked at the handle and flung open his door. It careened back and hit the limit of its range with a loud bang. He jumped out.

Angela leaned forward anxiously. "Where are you going?" She realized she had waited just a little bit too long; she should have been nice. All the girls wanted him, she was out of her league, and she knew he knew.

He didn't answer, he slammed his door shut. The dust on the dashboard jumped. She could hear his boots crunch on the gravel. He walked around the back and opened the hatch, and started dragging suitcases out, dropping them on the ground. Then he pulled out his sleeping bag and unrolled it and spread it out. He heaved himself up, kicked off his boots, and lay down.

"What are you doing?"

"What does it look like I'm doing." His voice was muffled in the quilting.

"Well, I'm not coming to join you." She peered around, hoping he would insist.

"Suit yourself," he said. Soon he was snoring.

Huffily, she got out of the car. She imagined when he woke and found her gone, he would panic and then they would make up. She walked along the road. It was hot, very hot, but not as hot as earlier. It was actually a lot more pleasant outside than being inside the air-conditioned car. She had set a schedule to conserve gas, ten minutes on, an hour off, but it wasn't pleasant either way.

Pink and yellow streaks were beginning to smudge the sky just above the horizon. She strode purposefully, enjoying stretching out her legs after hours of being cramped in a limited space. Her new hiking boots were surprisingly as comfortable as pillows, and the red dirt felt solid and good beneath her feet. She took deep breaths, savoring the pristine air, pure now it was still and the dust had settled. She gazed about her. Flaxen spinifex tufts spread as far as the eye could see. She watched as the sun slipped lower, taking with it the fading day, and the sky changed slowly to deep crimson. It was strangely, eerily quiet. Then a faint chirp, then another, and suddenly the owls began their evening concert. She stopped, listening. Every few moments new voices filled the air, a low-pitched *ooom-ooom-ooom* providing the bass, a repetitive one-note *book-book-book* kept the beat, and then a rapid strident *waark waark waark* burst in with a solo, to be followed by a low-key purring *mmmm* chorus. Then suddenly there was a discordant and hollow *chonk-chonk-chonk* which didn't fit in anywhere, like the tuba that had lost its music, and that made her laugh. She wanted to run right back to the car and share the concert with Eugene. But out of the corner of her eye she caught sight of a movement on the road. In the half-light she thought she could see dark figures up ahead, a small group moving quietly across the track. She wanted to call out, but the figures disappeared silently into the bush.

She ran back down the road and banged on the side of the car.

"Eugene! Eugene! Wake up! There's people here!"

He stirred sleepily. "Hmmm? What people?"

"There were people on the road. Just ahead."

"What kind of people?"

"Aborigines, I think."

"Oh." He lay back down, yawning. "Well, do they know how to fix a car engine? Fat lot of good they'd be to us. They'd just want something."

"But they know how to survive out here."

"No, they don't. They know how to survive on the dole is all they know."

"That's not fair. Anyway, the government is going to give them back their land."

"Why?"

"Because it's their ancestral land is why."

"Huh!" he said.

Angela frowned at him. "I thought you wanted to be a poverty lawyer, helping the downtrodden and all that."

"Yeah, well we all had to say that to get in. By the second year, we were all applying to the biggest corporate firms on the planet."

His feet were sticking out, he was too tall to sleep full length in the back. He had the A/C running full blast, with the hatch wide open. Angela ran to shut off the engine. The fuel gauge was down to less than a quarter.

Eugene looked at his watch and sat up. "We've been here a long time," he said. "Do we have any sandwiches?"

Angela opened the Esky and started lifting out Tupperware. "Where's the water?" she said, puzzled.

Eugene was silent, busy lacing up his boots.

"Where's all the water?" Angela said again. "There were four bottles of water in here."

Eugene climbed down and made a big issue of shaking out his bedroll and folding it.

Angela looked at him. "Eugene…?"

"Well, I drank it, so what. Someone will be along soon. Don't make such a big deal."

"How will someone be along? We haven't seen a car the whole time we've been stuck here."

"Because *we* came, didn't we? This is the route to Ayers, stupid. Of course someone will be along."

He tossed his sleeping bag in the car and opened a Tupperware box. He bit into a sandwich.

Angela couldn't let it go. "We were going to ration the water, remember?"

Eugene was chewing. He said through a mouthful, "You were going to get another case."

"No, *you* were. I got the spare gas tank filled. *You* were going to get the water."

Eugene popped the rest of the sandwich into his mouth. "Well, I misunderstood. So sue me. Ha ha, lawyer joke."

Angela picked up the Tupperware box and turned it upside down. "You took the last sandwich?"

Eugene clapped his hands to shake off the crumbs. "You shoulda told me sooner, don't you think? How was I to know it was the last one. I don't even like ham, remember? I told you that."

Angela said, "That didn't stop you eating it. I got the ham for me, so you already ate all yours?"

Eugene turned his back to her and fiddled with the laces on his boots. Angela watched him, knowing he felt cornered and was buying time.

She said sarcastically, "Planning to walk back to Coober Pedy, are you?"

Eugene couldn't think of anything to say. In such a situation, law school had taught him to throw out anything he could to obfuscate the issue. "We passed the rabbit fence just back down the road," he said.

"And we need to know that because …?"

"Because you know people had to build it."

"Of course people had to build it, but that was 80 years ago, it doesn't mean there's any people there now. Besides, it's called the dingo fence now."

"Yes, but people have to come and maintain it, don't they? Duh." He made it sound like a gotcha.

"What? Maybe once in 20 years somebody comes by to check it. You're going to walk 200 miles back there and wait 20 years, Eugene?"

He didn't reply. Angela couldn't stop herself. She said bitterly, "You never have any plans. You never have any ideas. You are never prepared, are you, Eugene? You have always just left it to me."

Offense is the best defense. Eugene stood up and whirled to face his wife.

"Yeah, and you always know best, don't you," he sneered. "You don't even have a degree, but boy you sure do know fucking everything, don't you. Have you ever stopped criticizing me? Hmm? Ever? I mean have you ever once not taken a dig at me?"

Angela didn't speak. Eugene set his feet wide and put his hands on his hips. He was happy to demonstrate how law school had made him able to beat her down with a good argument. He raised his voice. "Well, I hope you are happy now. You got us into this. *I* didn't want to come here, but I did what *you* wanted. *I* wanted to go to a civilized place with my friends, but you couldn't allow *that*, could you!"

Angela said nothing.

Sensing victory, Eugene went in for the kill with his grand summation. "So you had to have us drive 469 miles through bone-dry empty desert to Ayers. So now, Miss Smarty Pants, you tell me, you're so clever, you just tell me what we're going to do next."

He looked triumphant, smug. His voice had been satisfyingly loud and forceful, he had silenced and cowed her, he had cleverly shifted the blame to her. He looked at her, waiting for her to beg and plead and try to get back into his good graces, like she always did.

Angela didn't say anything. She pointed. Eugene turned his head.

Silent figures, a small band of dark men, their faces distinct in the light of the open hatch, stood quietly watching.

A DAY ON THE RIVER

Five men huddled in the pit they had dug in the sand. One of them muttered, "Fuck this."

"Bertrand, what's next?" said Prejean, his voice shaky with the cold.

The night was deepening and all they had were the clothes on their backs. They rubbed their hands together and slapped their arms and chests to keep warm. The crater in the earth gave them some protection against the wind and from the occasional drones that buzzed overhead.

"Ask Vincent, he knows the area," said Bertrand. He had a satchel under his arm. He shifted the weight of it to rest on his considerable belly, but he didn't loosen his grip. "Hey Vinny, what now? The drones have us pinned down."

Vincent was silent, looking up at the sky. The faint light flashed above them and disappeared, the sound fading.

"They have about 30 hours of juice, we can wait it out," he said.

The others looked at each other. They weren't happy.

"We dug our own grave," wailed Dave. "We're sitting in our own grave. What if they start shooting?"

Stan, the young local river guide, looked about to cry.

"Drones don't have guns," said Vincent.

"Yeah, but the FBI owns the drones, and they have guns. I'm outta here." Dave suddenly jumped up and scrambled out of the pit, clawed his way up the riverbank, and vanished into the darkness. The others watched him go.

Bertrand eased his bulk over, taking up most of the newly vacated space. "Good riddance. We can split three ways now." He said it as though young Stan wasn't sitting right there and couldn't count.

Prejean finally spoke. "Look, I ain't planning to lie here like a target freezing my balls off for 30 hours. I say we should all make a run for it like Dave."

Vincent said, "You need to be patient. Besides, Bertrand's ankle is busted ..." His voice was drowned out by another overhead buzz.

"I don't feel like being patient, and I'm cold." Prejean tucked his neck down deeper into his light parka and wrapped his arms tightly about him. He wiggled his rump to dig himself in deeper. Young Stan burrowed into him like a puppy seeking warmth.

"Of course it's cold. It's November on the Columbia. Besides, DB did it in November, didn't he?" Vincent kept his voice very even, very calm.

"We could wait for daylight, there may be more to find around here." That was Bertrand again. "They never found the parachute. They never found the attaché case with the bomb."

"If there ever was a bomb."

"Yeah, well we only looked in one place. What if there's more? We could look and see if there's more when it gets light." That was Bertrand again. He had twisted his ankle jumping into the hole, and it would be to his advantage to stay there longer and let it heal a bit.

Vincent said, "Yeah, but I watched the old guy, and he watched the FBI, so he knew where they looked, and he knew that wasn't where it was. He figured out the most likely place."

"When did he die?"

"Last week. The drone spotted him at the bottom of one of the holes he dug." A buzz overhead stopped all conversation for a moment. When it passed Vincent said, "I watched him, I knew he had to be getting close. And, bingo, I hit pay-dirt." He paused, glancing around. "Well, *we* hit pay-dirt. I couldn't have done it without you guys."

"We wouldn't have let you do it without us guys!" Prejean snickered. The others laughed. "We spotted you digging, Vinny. Knew it had to be something good. Just out rafting innocently down the Columbia with our river guide young Stan here, and there's this yokel on the bank digging like a frenzied ferret."

Bertrand shifted to a more comfortable position. "Well, we knew you was onto something. With all our added muscle we helped you find what you was looking for, am I right? So all good, right?"

They laughed again. Vincent said nothing. It wasn't a surprise that he had been watched, he half expected it. He pretended to be busy scanning the sky.

Prejean looked up too. "What if the drone's not the FBI. Might be another treasure-hunter, one with no scruples."

"Yeah, well," said Vinny. "Like I said, I watched the old guy, so no reason why somebody else wasn't watching him too. But most people lost interest back in 2016. The Feds said they wouldn't be looking full-time anymore, they had other cases to work on, but they said if anyone found anything to let them know."

They all laughed heartily at that, even young Stan, and it took the edge off the tension.

Vincent said, "Look guys. The old man led us right to it, it's a gift, so at least we can be patient a few more hours, OK?"

One of the men began grumbling. Prejean punched the satchel in Bertrand's lap. "Why don't we just split the loot and run for it. We need to head in different directions. The drone can't follow us all."

Bertrand said, "I can't run, and you ain't leaving me here." His arms tightened around the satchel.

There was silence. The wind nudged at the edges of the group, and they instinctively pulled closer together. The sky was black, just a canopy of velvet with pinholes of flickering light.

To kill time, Prejean said, "Vinny, how long you been looking?"

"Well, I was here when I was a kid. We were camping, and we saw all the people digging. My parents figured it out. Somebody found some bills, they were all torn and beat up because they were just loose, but the FBI matched the serial numbers."

"Didn't your folks want to stay and keep looking? Obviously the bills fell out of a satchel like this one here." Bertrand patted the bag.

"Nah. I went swimming and we picked up driftwood for a fire, and I scratched around a bit. We went home the next day."

"Didn't you ever want to come back and look for more?"

"Nah. I read that people kept swarming this area, looking, then I forgot about it for years. Till I saw the old guy on TV. I mean why would you go clucking your head off on TV that you know where it's buried?"

Silence settled on the group. Suddenly, the familiar buzz came up over the cliff, and the men crouched down lower, hiding their faces.

Young Stan whimpered, "Go away, go away!"

Prejean muttered, "I feel like I'm being hunted like a dog."

"Shut up!" hissed Bertrand. He was afraid the drone could pick up sound. The buzz became louder, hovering directly overhead. It was as though the drone could see them huddled there and was taking names. Then it continued on, disappearing over the far riverbank.

There was nothing more to say. The men fell silent. There was peace in the sky. The wind had died down and the water lapped rhythmically at the bank. The hours churned on, and around midnight Prejean sat up carefully so as not to disturb the others and looked around. There was no moon. He glanced downstream. The raft was snuggled into a cove in the river, overhanging rock keeping it well hidden from prying eyes in the sky. He eased his backside up onto the sand and hoisted himself out of the pit. He waited, watching, listening. Bertrand tossed fitfully, his swollen ankle pulled up protectively under him, his hands still clutching the satchel. Vincent's chin was on his chest, rasping snores escaping from his open mouth. The youngster, Stan, was curled up in fetal position lost to the world.

Prejean pulled his legs up cautiously, and when the others didn't stir, he began to crawl toward the raft. He dislodged it from the rocks and moved it to the edge of the river and looped the tow rope around a driftwood log. He crept quietly back to the group huddled in the pit. He stood above

Bertrand, and with one quick movement snatched the satchel out of his arms and ran back to the raft.

The shouts of the men on the beach pierced the night. Prejean tossed the satchel into the raft, yanked the rope loose, grabbed an oar and pushed the raft out into midstream. He reached for the second oar. In the dark, he didn't even notice Stan sitting quietly in the bow. With one mighty swipe of the long-shaft paddle, Stan knocked Prejean clean over the side and into the swirling water. Prejean reached frantically for the wrap-around guide rope but came up clutching air, and with a howl, he was carried off into the darkness.

Stan steadied the raft, tucked the satchel safely under his seat, and began rhythmic oaring. He expertly maneuvered the Triton into the swift current and headed downstream.

"Traitor! Traitor!" screamed Bertrand. The echo bounced off the canyon walls, mocking him.

T-R-A-I-T-O-R   t-r-a-i-t-o-r   t-r-a-i-t-o-r

The sound trailed away, muffled by the rising river mist. Vincent found that he could stretch his legs all the way across the pit. "Where's Stan?" He peered into the dark. "Young Stan's gone?"

Bertrand rasped morosely, "Probably ran off. Like Dave."

There was a pause, each man sliding deep into his own thoughts. Suddenly, another drone burst into the sky above them. Bertrand ducked down and tugged at his jacket and tried to pull it up over his head.

Vincent watched him, and when the noise faded, he said, "Bertrand, it doesn't matter anymore. We don't have anything they want now, do we?" He started to laugh. But then he became aware that he was laughing alone, and even to him, his last ha-ha sounded very forced. The man opposite him didn't join in. Bertrand wasn't laughing. In fact, Bertrand wasn't saying anything at all. Vincent felt a chill run through him, an unease that he couldn't put a name to.

After several minutes he said, making his voice very jovial, "Well, no need to stay here any longer, is there?" He scrambled to his feet and yawned and feigned a long, exaggerated stretch. "Well," he said, and took a step toward the edge of the pit. He hoisted one leg up onto the rim and was about to pull up the other, when a beefy hand shot out, grabbed his foot, and pulled him back.

"You ain't going nowhere!" Bertrand barked.

Vincent was slammed down face first into the cold river mud and pinned there by Bertrand's heavy leg across his back. Just then another drone whipped up over them, as though it had been tossed into the air from the nearest riverbank. It hovered, its buzz muted by the swirling mist. When it passed, neither man spoke for a while.

Vincent tried to spit the sand out of his mouth. "What's the matter?" he said at last. "We need to get you some attention for that ankle. Wouldn't it be good if you were found now, hmm?"

A long silence. Finally Bertrand said, "I ain't going back."

"Back where?" said Vincent. He twisted his head to look up at Bertrand. "I am going back to Virginia, that's where I'm going, just as soon as I get out of here …" He heard himself chattering, but his mind was churning totally disconnected from his tongue.

"To prison," said Bertrand.

"Oh, uh, prison." Vincent paused. He dropped his head back onto the sand. "Um, had a check or two bounce, did you?"

"Murder."

"Oh," said Vincent. "Mur – der." His mouth had difficulty forming the word. The conversation had run its course. At least for Vincent. He didn't want to, or need to, know anything else. He eyed the rim of the pit, measuring the distance. If only a leg the size of a driftwood log wasn't pinning him to the ground.

"It was self-defense."

"Oh, I am sure it was," said Vincent quickly. "Uh-huh, no doubt in my mind. At all."

"Prejean and me was cellies."

"Oh, cell-mates," said Vincent. "Well, it's always nice to travel with a friend." He tried to ease one arm free of the human log.

"Now he's run off with all the money."

"Yes, that was unkind of him," Vincent said. He got his left arm free. "If you could just … my other arm, you know."

Bertrand seemed not to hear. "We busted out together, me and him."

Just then another drone darted up. Vincent's brain flashed dully on the sudden increase in drone surveillance. He considered waving his free arm but thought better of it. His face ached, his neck ached, his back ached, and his trapped right arm ached. When the sky had cleared, he said, "You probably know where Prejean is headed, right? I mean you guys must have had a plan, right? I can help you find him."

"We saw the old guy on TV," Bertrand muttered.

"Oh, just like I did. You saw him on TV, and just like I did, you decided to come here and, um, help him look?"

"Prejean and me, we both had the same thought, that's our ticket to freedom, we just got to get our butts down there and find the old fool and get the money."

"Well, you certainly made it," Vincent said, his voice hearty with approval. "So did you come from anywhere around here?"

"Canada."

"Oh, Canada, of course, I should have known, your names, Prejean, Bertrand. I've always wanted to visit Canada."

"Cellies all these years, and he betrays me."

"Yes, that is disappointing, isn't it," said Vincent.

"A guard got killed."

"Oh." Vincent was thinking nervously about how the bodies were piling up. He said reassuringly, "Well, he got in your way, right?"

"It was self-defense," Bertrand said.

"Oh, quite, I can see that …"

Just then, a shout came from the cliff top.

Bertrand's head whipped around. "That sounded like Dave," he said, eyes straining to see through the mist.

Vincent could hardly keep the joy from his voice. "Oh, Dave's back?" he burbled, trying to make it sound casual, like Dave had just popped out to the store for milk.

With one ear buried in the sand, he couldn't be sure, but it sounded like a lot more than one set of feet scrambling down the bank. He was right. Twelve troopers accompanied Dave. They swarmed onto the beach crouched low, rifles at the ready, and approached the pit in the sand.

NO GOD KNOWS THIS PLACE

I remember how the derricks rose like boney black fingers, reaching out from the bowels of the earth toward a steel-grey sky. Men scurried like columns of ants in and out of the bottomless pits. The Saar had always been a harsh place, and the mines as dangerous as coal mines everywhere, with explosions, cave-ins, fires, and poisoned air. But the Saarland mines presented the additional hazard of being dug into sandstone. The sandstone layers covering the mine tunnels often split and collapsed, trapping all beneath, and creating shock waves that caused the ground at the surface to heave and shake. Monstrous cracks appeared in town buildings, bricks dropped from the church steeple, smokestacks toppled, and houses buckled and sank against their neighbors, the whole row falling like dominoes. The aura of imminent tragedy hung forever like a shroud in the gritty air.

Every day we were braced, listening for the scream of the siren, dreading the knock at the door that announced that our lives would be shattered forever by the loss of a loved one.

My father had worked in the mine since he was a boy, first as a miner's helper, then as a miner, and as with many locals, mining ran back through countless generations of his family. It was all he had ever known. He left the house before dawn, riding his bicycle to the pithead to pick up his lamp and gear, and we would not see him again until well after dark. He spent twelve hours a day down in the mine.

His ice-blue eyes, so pale they were almost colorless, were startling in their contrast to his blackened face. Coal dust was ingrained into the deep creases of his neck, into every crack and pore of his hands, creeping like leprosy up the work-coarsened wrists that jutted below the sleeves of his jacket.

During the meagre time he was at home he seldom spoke. He did little other than stare silently out the window. I would hover nearby, keeping very quiet, not wanting to disturb him, just happy to be in his company. To me he was a hero.

On rare occasions my father would be gripped by rage, fueled by something intangible, as though the fear that always hung thick about the town had seeped into his very bones. He would suddenly and unexpectedly bellow his hidden pain like an animal inescapably and permanently trapped. My mother's mouth would droop, and her eyes would grow wide and moist as her trembling fingers plucked helplessly at her apron. As suddenly as it started, my father's voice would fall still, and then, as though ashamed to have exposed the harrowing anguish that consumed him, and fearing to contaminate me with his despair, my father would stumble out the door, back into the foul air.

Sunday was his one day off, and he tried to make it special. On Sundays, when the townspeople were at church, and the sky was not too overcast, and the weather was not too foggy, damp or cold, he would take me out to the hills. I would sit on his handlebars squealing with delight as he peddled as fast as he could, bouncing with joyful abandon along the rough country roads. At the hilltop, he pointed out the lush stretches of forest that spread far beyond the bleak desolation of our town.

Of course, he incurred the wrath of our neighbors for not being a devout God-fearing, church-going worshiper. They asserted that we should all pray hard on Sundays to appease, placate, and garner as much goodwill as we could from Heaven.

My father told them, "In this place, you will find no favor with God."

One Sunday was different. My father called me to him. Instead of the expected trip to the hill-top, he sat me down and quietly told me I would be going away. That was all he said. I was stunned and bewildered, and pleaded with him, what have I done, why would you send your only child away, if you are angry just spank me, but please don't send me away.

My Oma came for me. Oma was a tall stout woman with a billowing bosom that rested upon her ample stomach. When she arrived, she did not speak to me condescendingly, or bend down to greet me at eye level pretending that we were equals, as grownups usually do. Instead, she regarded me thoughtfully from her great height. Her eyes were the same piercing blue as my father's.

Oma had left our town when the mine made her a widow. It was very difficult for her to return now. She had long ago settled in a village in the south. The long train journey must have been exhausting for her, by then she was quite elderly. I slept almost all the way. Our train shuddered to a halt at her station, and Oma picked up my small suitcase and marched along the cobbled streets to her cottage. I scurried breathlessly on my short legs to keep up. I felt as though I was following a mighty mountain.

My Oma stood towering and solid. Like my father, she was a woman of very few words, but she was a fortress, strong, fearless, safe, and she offered me another world. Where my Oma lived the air was crisp and clear, the sun shone, and birds sang in green leafy trees. But my heart ached, and I was numb with a sense of betrayal, and with homesickness for my father.

The day came when Oma got word from the Saar that the siren had wailed and acrid smoke had spiraled up once again over the rooftops, and that day, the dreaded knock was at the door of my parents' house. My Oma, grim-faced and resolute, took me on the long train journey back home to lay her son to rest.

The atmosphere in town had never been pleasant. Local people resented the mine owners who continued to operate, knowing that the tremors endangered not only the miners, but everyone in town. If an earthquake had struck, they would accept that because it was an unavoidable act of God. But this destruction was man-made, deliberate, greedy, and immoral. There were several marches and protests. Some shopkeepers demonstrated their disapproval in the only way they could, by refusing to serve the miners. Some miners had even been attacked in town. But in this time of catastrophe, they came together as one to honor the men who had just lost their lives. People in their black clothes filed slowly toward the mine, a long dark column of grief, to pay tribute to their own.

My mother did not participate. Years of fear had hollowed her out. Her eyes were unseeing, empty. The mine company had already taken back our house, and my mother was admitted to State care. There was nothing left for me to do except to say goodbye to my father. The three bodies had been lost far too deep in the mine to be retrieved. My father would have been satisfied; remaining there with his two friends was preferable to a formal church burial in the cemetery.

My Oma, now bereft of both a husband and a son, walked at my side. The mine gate was high and imposing, an arch formed by an intricate lacework of wrought iron. It was closed and locked, the mine temporarily shut down, and eerily quiet save for the shuffling of mourners' feet.

I looked through the railing at the buildings that had ruled our lives, and there, leaning against the red brick wall, was my father's bicycle. I had not cried when I was banished to my Oma's house, I had not cried when they took my mother to the State hospital, but I cried now to see my father's bicycle, ignored, unneeded and abandoned, waiting in vain for him to return.

THE MILLION DOLLAR DUCHESS

T he land was a gift to the Duke from a grateful Crown. The War of the Spanish Succession had raged for three years. With the final English victory at Blenheim in 1704, Queen Anne rewarded her army well. The Duke had somehow helped in the military triumphs against the French and Bavarians, saved Vienna, and prevented the collapse of the Grand Alliance. His compensation was generous for his services.

The Duke set about building a castle, one of the largest in England, on his magnificent new piece of land. Owing to his war travels, its theatrical style had numerous inspirations. There was of course a hint of gentle English classical rhythms, but those were very much overwhelmed by the exuberance and style of Italian and French baroque palaces. The general response to the result was mixed. It was described by the more charitable observers as a cross between a mausoleum and a monastery.

The courtyard created an impressively framed approach to the massive entrance portico. There were prominent towers at the four corners of the main building, each embellished by gilded and painted statues of exotic beasts, and each apex was capped with elaborate sculptured finials. A clerestoried Great Hall led to a long picture gallery, a library, a vast dining hall, a salon, and a spacious ballroom with a musicians' loft above. A wide elaborately carved staircase led to upper floors. The interior decoration and fittings were lavishly completed with door and window frames of marble. The colorful ceiling and wall fresco paintings glorified England's battles, England's successful battles, that is. There were said to be 187 rooms in the main house. It became the home of the Duke's family and the seat of the Dukedom for the next 200 years.

Those two centuries weighed heavily upon the estate. The present Duke noticed the peeling paint, decaying stonework, and something had happened to the roof in the last few heavy winter storms causing the upstairs bedroom chandeliers to be ringed with unsightly damp stains. Rats had compromised a section of the ballroom floor, and just yesterday a gargoyle had fallen off a turret and crashed to the ground dangerously close to the Duke on his morning walk.

The reason for this neglect was simple. The British aristocracy had always relied upon rents collected from tenant farmers to maintain the splendor of their great country estates. But with the onset of the Industrial Revolution, the Duke's tenant farmers had run off to work in town factories. This left a considerable hole in the Duke's source of income, since the true distinction between English classes was that gentlemen of the aristocracy did not work.

But luckily, with the advent of the 1900s Gilded Age, it was brought to the Duke's attention that advantageous arranged marriages had become common. The Duke could gild his castle, replenish his income, and save his ancestral home, invigorated by a surprising source. Just across the ocean were people who, unlike him, had worked very hard. Unfortunately, they were far less cultured, but that perhaps could be overlooked.

The formal gardens and the surrounding parkland, a crucial part of the estate design, provided an impressive setting for the main house. Across that parkland (which badly needed mowing), at the window of the charming (but crumbling) guest cottage, Ida Krakenbush was gazing at the castle.

"Whatta white elephant," she said. Her voice was pure Bronx.

Someone scratched timidly at the door.

"Servants!" Ida muttered. And she yelled, "What?"

"I have a basin of hot water and some towels like you wanted, and the doctor is here."

The doctor cleared his throat loudly to confirm that.

The young woman lying on the bed squirmed. Her wrists were tied to the bedpost with silk stockings. She looked nervously toward the door.

"But I love Alphonso," she whined to her mother.

"Impossible, he's a waiter," Ida snapped, and then shouted at the door, "Give us a moment, will ya?"

"Untie me," the girl pleaded.

"No, you keep running away. You've already tried to elope once with that immigrant dirt bag."

"Alphonso isn't a dirt bag."

"I should have him shot for ruining our chances like this."

"No, no don't do that! Besides, we can't elope since he's still back in the Bronx, but I still won't marry the Duke."

"Yes, you will. You'll be a Duchess, and I'll be a Dowager Duchess. Or a Mother Duchess. Or Duchess Royal. Anyway, Mrs. Caroline Astor of New York, now you will *have* to invite me to your grand balls. Do you know she even called me a conniving social climber? She snubs me like I'm some kinda reptile just crawled up on Ellis Island. Well, we'll see about *that* when there's a Duchess in the family."

"It's all I have to remind me of Alphonso."

"Like I said, it's up to you. Nobody's forcing you. But I do not feel well, you know my heart is weak, I may not survive. It's up to you, but I'm growing faint."

She dabbed a handkerchief at her temples.

Hesitant tapping came again at the door. "Ma'am, the hot water is getting cold. And the doctor said he is very busy."

The doctor cleared his throat impatiently to prove that.

Ida said to her daughter, "It won't hurt. Lots of women do it." She patted the girl's knee. "It might sting a bit, is all."

"But I love Alphonso, and it's a part of him."

"Yeah, right. Well, I feel very dizzy, I think my heart is going …"

"Oh Mama, don't say that, please don't become ill."

"Well, then, perhaps I will get better if you do this now. I can let the doctor in, we can get it over with. Then you can marry the Duke with a clear conscience."

"His breath smells."

"Then feed him parsley."

"The castle is cold and draughty, the roof leaks and there's no electricity or running hot water."

"I know Darling, and that is why he is marrying you. Your Daddy's million-dollar dowry will save his rotting castle. Then you'll live like royalty." She sniffed. "Take that, Mrs. High Society Caroline Astor! Like making a million bucks manufacturing railroad ties gets you nothing."

The tapping at the door was more urgent. "Ma'am, the water is cold, and the doctor has to leave."

There was the sound of footsteps receding.

Ida fanned herself vigorously with her handkerchief.

"Now look what you've done. You've missed your one chance to be respectable." She threw herself into a chair. "Now Mrs. Astor will never invite me, I'll never meet New York society, and oh, if only I wasn't so ill. I am feeling more and more ill, you know."

"Oh, Mama, please, please stop. OK, I'll marry him, I'll marry the Duke. But not the other thing."

The girl turned her face to the wall.

Ida worked her white hanky. "Well, I suppose I can let out the dress, and we'll just have to tell the Duke it was an immaculate conception."

OLD TIMES

My family didn't really celebrate anything. Birthdays, anniversaries, Easter, Guy Fawkes, Harvest Festival, and certainly not Christmas. Well, Christmas a bit. My mother went through the motions, resentful, put-upon, slamming pots on the stove. I wondered why she even bothered. My father came to the table in his underwear, silently wolfed down whatever was put in front of him, then slammed his chair against the wall and went back to the television. I exclaimed how good the ham tasted, but my voice was hollow, it was a silly thing to say, today had nothing to do with the ham. My mother's face remained a study in victimhood. We couldn't wash the dishes; and we were desperate not to scrape our chairs on the linoleum floor. We had to wait until we heard him snoring. We couldn't talk above a whisper, if indeed there was anything to say, in case it disturbed my father. So the three of us sat in silence, leftover food congealing on the plates, wishing we were spending Christmas anywhere else, with anyone else.

Our portion of the house was the back half, the kitchen, one bathroom, the room where my mother and I slept, and a small utility room that was my brother's bedroom. The rest was my father's area, off-limits to us, where the living room had carpets, a sofa, a fireplace, large windows with lace curtains, and the television set. Once in a long while, my father would invite us in to watch a particular TV program. My mother, brother and I would sit awkwardly on the couch, smiling hard to show our gratitude. My father would turn up the sound to suit himself and swivel the television toward his armchair. The three of us would crane uncomfortably from the couch, unable to really see the screen, our ears assaulted by the volume. When the show was over, my father would simply turn off the TV and without a word, plod across the hall to his bedroom. My mother, brother and I would take a moment to recover, and then silently file out to the back of the house where we belonged.

Most of the time my father stayed in bed all day, reading and chain-smoking. My mother took his meals in to him on a tray. The three of us were thankful to eat in the kitchen without him. If for some reason he did join us, the tension was thick, palpable. He shoveled food into his mouth and rambled on and on, words and crumbs tumbling out, describing whatever he was currently reading. His interests were broad, he talked of Marco Polo's travels, of Samuel Pepys essays, of the bombing of Hiroshima, of the Egyptian pyramids, of British rule in Hong Kong. Other times he would reminisce about getting into fights at the coal mines in south Wales, or how he had punched a teacher at his school and been expelled, or of his unruly behavior in the Army. He was an intelligent man, but he had never fit in anywhere. He was never in the kitchen to share a family meal with us, there was no connection, no chit-chat or general conversation. He was there merely to take advantage of a captive audience.

My brother nervously crammed food into his mouth but was too stressed to swallow, and his cheeks bulged. My mother's mouth twisted downward, her face sour and her eyes flat, expressionless. She said, "Oh, mmm," from time to time, pretending to be interested as he rambled on. When my father mindlessly dug into an apple pie intended to be shared by all of us, she merely looked upset, but said nothing as he gobbled the whole thing. When he was finished, he left abruptly, and though we inwardly sighed with relief, the room still contained the aura of his toxic presence, and we dared not even exchange glances.

I was always half-listening for his footsteps, mentally gauging through the walls where he might be. I could practically determine the state of his mood from the heft of his tread. When his footsteps were regularly paced and even, I could relax a little. But when they were thundering, oppressive, unbalanced, my stomach cramped in fear. On those days he would burst through the door into the kitchen, shouting unintelligibly, and start punching whoever was nearest. I would jump to shield my brother, even though he was taller than I, as he stood transfixed, trembling, eyes wide and terrified. It used to be my mother who went down, but lately he had punched me. When my father had gone my mother would transfer her hopelessness to me, viciously blaming me for his mood, hissing punishing words at me.

The Vietnam War was still raging. By now it was common knowledge that America was fudging the casualty numbers. Prime Minister Robert Menzies had announced in Parliament that Australia would send combat troops to Vietnam, including immigrants like us, setting the conscription age at 20. On the morning of my brother's 20th birthday, my father strode into the kitchen. Our family barely *acknowledged* birthdays, let alone celebrated them, so we nearly jumped out of our skins when my father suddenly loomed through the doorway. He laid a fat envelope on the kitchen table. We stood rigid, like stone pillars, fearful for whatever might come next.

My father turned to my brother. "I want you to leave for England right away. Here's your British passport, you can live there. England's government had the sense to resist American pressure to join the war. I will not allow you to be sent to an insane war that has no purpose." It took a moment to absorb. In retrospect it wasn't a total surprise to me, my father had once briefly mentioned his wretchedness on the beach at Dunkirk, how the English soldiers waited hours while German planes screamed overhead strafing them, how they had to climb over the bloodied bodies of their fallen comrades to get to the little fishing boats that took them home. My brother timidly opened the envelope and counted out the bank notes. I said quickly, "He can travel with Josh and Billy next door, they are going to England for their gap year before uni."

I knew there was no chance my brother would go to college, he had dropped out of high school, he didn't have what it took. Or perhaps he did, and the nerve-wracking atmosphere at home had killed any potential. Either way, a college exemption was not in his future. I helped him pack. The night before he left was New Year's, and there was a big send-off for Josh and Billy at the pub. I didn't tell my parents, neither was comfortable around other people.

The noise was deafening as people yelled and danced to the raucous band. My brother and I sat quietly in a corner, a world away from the party atmosphere. The crowd serenaded Josh and Billy, Auld Lang Syne, farewell but come back soon, don't let old times be forgotten.

"Let old times be forgotten," I said to my brother. "Don't come back."

There was nothing more to be said.

TWELVE MONKEYS AND A BANJO

Mr. Spell's vibrant paintings gave an outlet to his rich imagination, bringing the vivid images in his head to dramatic life. Intricate shapes and brilliant colors poured from his brushes onto his flamboyant canvases. He could have set the art world on fire if he had chosen to paint realistic landscapes or presidential portraits, but his taste ran to fanciful jungle foliage and primitive cartoon animals.

Mr. Spell's short stature allowed adults, and even some children, a bird's eye view of his shiny head. He had a button nose, chubby cheeks, bowed legs, and a very strong stutter which tested the patience of listeners, who grew restless and tried to finish his sentences. But it did not deter those who came to buy his paintings. Some lucky ones who had been able to flee the disintegrating streets and growing crime remembered Mr. Spell's imaginative paintings, and when they had disposable income, they bravely returned to buy his pictures. Others, who had nothing but a big appetite for his fantasies, came just to look.

One such was Miss Tree. She came from her house four doors away to feast her eyes on one painting in particular. Mr. Spell was finally moved to present it to her as a gift, partly because she had been his mother's friend, and partly because her jangling jewelry gave him a headache. The local children called her Miss Christmas Tree. She repaid him handsomely with homemade casseroles and butter cookies. Miss Tree also always brought Lady a few dog treats left over from Guacamole, her Chihuahua.

As with many of us who were not created in the perfect human image, Mr. Spell had an uncanny connection with animals, especially with his faithful golden retriever. Lady took responsibility for her own daily walk, sensing that her master's poor bent legs might not be up to it. She set off briskly at precisely 9 o'clock every morning, and she always followed the same route, and she was gone for exactly 45 minutes and 15 seconds. She passed the Watson house whose eye-catching color was due to a blow-out year-end sale of lilac paint. She passed the Marshall's sagging porch which creaked even on a windless day. She passed the Jones' white cat, which observed her through golden-eyed slits. When she came to Miss Tree's house, the one where Mr. Spell's painting now resided, Guacamole yelped shrill braggadocio from behind the safety of a picture window. Lady always ignored him.

However, the day came when Lady was passing Miss Tree's house, and Guacamole was not at the window yelping and performing vertical jumps. Lady paused and stood looking through the garden gate. The lace curtain framing the dark room was still and undisturbed. Lady waited a few minutes before going on her way. The next morning Miss Tree's big picture window was again silent, dark and empty. Lady ventured a quick bark, very low-key and dignified so as not to disturb the neighbors. But no Guacamole appeared. Something was clearly amiss. Lady pondered the mystery for a moment. Then she made a decision and ran home.

Mr. Spell looked up from his painting in surprise. He said, "B-b-b-b-a-c-k   a-l-r-r-r-r-e-a-d-y?"

Lady nudged his knee. She had never before disturbed him while he was working, and Mr. Spell's eyebrows shot up, his brush poised in mid-air. Lady ran out to the street, looking over her shoulder to make sure Mr. Spell followed. And follow he did, still in his apron, hobbling and wobbling, arms flailing for balance. The white cat abandoned her indifference and sat up eyes wide to watch. Mr. Watson glimpsed them from the window of his lilac house. The neighborhood may have been diminished, but not so the caring soul of its occupants, and Mr. Watson, who owned the only telephone on the street, immediately called the police.

Lady wasted no time. She ran through the gate of Miss Tree's neat garden and directly to the front door. She barked a little, but no Guacamole answered. Mr. Spell told Lady to wait there, and he ran around to the back. The kitchen door was ajar, its broken lock hanging. Miss Tree was sitting on the floor, her head in her hands. A hammer lay nearby, and cigarette butts littered the floor. Miss Tree had never been known to smoke. Drawers were gaping open; contents were dangling out all askew.

The police detective arrived and strode into the house, notebook at the ready. The photographer trotted in behind him and started work. Mr. Spell approached the detective.

"A p-p-p-p-i-c-t ..." he managed to say.

The detective cut him short. "Yes, he's taking pictures," he snapped, busily writing in his notebook.

Mr. Spell tried again. "M-m-m-m-i-s-s-s-s-ing p-p-p-p-i-c-t-t-t-t..."

The detective whirled on him. "Are you trying to tell us how to do our job?"

Mr. Spell pointed to a spot on the wall with an empty picture hanger, and tried again, "M-m-m-m-m-y p-p-p-p-p-i-c-t-t-t-u-r-e ..." The detective called to the police officer, and as though Mr. Spell's speech impediment made him deaf as well, said loudly, "Take charge of this man. He was first on the scene. The guilty often come back. And take his cigarette packet into evidence."

Mr. Spell motioned vigorously that he did not smoke, but he was by now getting in the way of the ambulance men. Mr. Watson and Lady were craning to see, barred from entry, but when the police officer left the porch to hustle Mr. Spell to the front room, Lady slipped in. She was very concerned. She put her head in Mr. Spell's lap and whimpered. And at the sound, who should slide out from under the couch? Guacamole. His head was hanging low, his eyes downcast, his tail between his trembling legs. The one and only time his yelping could have been of some help to his mistress, he had remained silent. He licked Lady's ankles.

When the detective was done with the kitchen, he transferred his attention to the living room. He asked Mr. Spell a lot of questions, scribbling in his notebook with excessive zeal. Mr. Spell wondered what on earth he could be writing, since he never managed to utter more than half of one word before being cut off. The detective snapped his notebook shut. Mr. Spell was allowed to go home. He was told sternly not to go anywhere, a request Mr. Spell agreed to easily since he had never been beyond his neighborhood in his life. He took Guacamole with him.

A few days later, while Miss Tree was recovering nicely in the hospital and Mr. Spell was just about to start to paint an identical picture to the one stolen from her, there was a knock at his door, and a lady with flaming red hair, a color certainly never seen in nature, came in and admired his paintings. She said that at the flea market on Tuesday, she had seen a painting that looked just like his style.

She said, "I really loved it, cute little monkeys, but the vendor wanted way too much for it. I asked if it was an original Henri Rousseau, you know the French post-impressionist painter that Picasso mentored? He said yes, but then I had to spell Rousseau for him."

Mr. Spell's ears pricked up, and he wrote on a piece of paper asking would she take him to the flea market. Hopefully the vendor and the picture would be there again.

The next Tuesday, Mr. Spell put on his best jacket and dropped some treats in his pocket for Lady and Guacamole. He went to the lilac house and told Mr. Watson the purpose of the flea market visit and asked him to please make a quick phone call. Mr. Watson made the call, and, eager to help, joined them in the red-haired lady's car. As luck would have it, the vendor was there, puffing away at a cigarette beneath a large No Smoking sign. Guacamole, who had been shamed and silent for his entire stay at Mr. Spell's house, suddenly started barking shrilly. In fact, his ear-splitting yelping caused people to look and point at that booth, so when the police showed up, in force and miraculously on time, they were able to quickly find their target. The vendor looked wildly about him, but Mr. Watson and Mr. Spell closed in on each side and Lady planted herself firmly behind him, leaving no avenue of escape.

The detective rushed up, all out of breath, and immediately noticed Mr. Spell. He shouted, "You were not supposed to go anywhere. Arrest him!" The vendor realized he was not the suspect, and was about to make a run for it, but Lady wasn't having that. She bit his ankle and he fell to the ground. Lady restrained the vendor, and Mr. Watson restrained the detective. He explained that the robbery evidence was all right there on the table, the big shiny brooches, necklaces, and rings that he had seen Miss Tree wear regularly.

Mr. Spell butted in and pointed to a picture lying half hidden under the jewelry.

He said, "I p-p-p-ain-t-t-t-ed   th-th-th-a …"

Mr. Watson confirmed to the detective that he knew the picture was the one that Mr. Spell had painted and had given to Miss Tree.

"Then he needs to identify the picture. If he really painted it, he would know what's in it." The detective picked up the picture and held it at an angle so Mr. Spell could not see it. He peered at it for a moment, then as though grilling a flagrantly guilty suspect, bellowed, "How many monkeys are in it?"

"T-t-t-t-…" Mr. Spell did his best.

The detective cut him off triumphantly. "Two? Wrong, so it's not your picture!"

"T-t-t-t-t-t-…" Mr. Spell tried again.

"Ten? Nope, good try, but wrong again. You are just wasting my time!" He tossed the painting to the police officer.

"Tut-tut-tut-tut-w-e-l-v-e!" Mr. Spell finally got it out. The police officer quickly counted. "Sir, there are twelve monkeys, he's right."

"Oh, that's just a good guess after three tries," the detective sneered.

"And a banjo!" Mr. Spell's stutter was gone in his excitement.

The police officer again studied the picture, then exclaimed, "He's right, it does have twelve monkeys and a banjo!"

The police officer beckoned his colleague, and they grabbed the vendor, still lying on the ground under Lady's watchful eye. They cuffed and pulled him to his feet. Guacamole continued to leap up and down, barking shrilly.

"The dog recognizes him," the police officer said helpfully as he led the vendor away.

The detective nodded at the table and said to no-one in particular, "Get that stuff down to the station." Clutching his aching temples, he wailed, "Oh, that damn dog ..." and he hurried out of earshot.

As officers began to box up Miss Tree's belongings, Mr. Spell reached over the table, and the red-haired lady got her painting.

MARIE-HÉLÈNE FOCQUET, SPY

There was a narrow river at the bottom of the steep and craggy valley. The guide explained there was no other way. The river was deep and ran fast, but he had made it across before, guiding others who were escaping. Her friends eased her down the cliff, careful not to put pressure on her wounds. They formed a human chain and handed her from one to the next across the gushing river, and they carried her all the way into Calais. Marie-Hélène was born there, she knew the seaport well, and she breathed in the familiar smell of the docks she had strolled when her legs and her body were strong. The guide whistled, and when a low whistle came in return, they motioned to her and helped her across the gangplank and hustled her aboard a fishing boat. The fishermen told her to lie down in a corner of the deck and be still. She fell into an exhausted sleep under a pile of stinking fishing nets.

She was awakened by the grating of the hull against a dock. They pulled away the fishing nets, and she blinked in the sudden light. A young man was standing on the dock, waving both arms. She waved back exuberantly. Happiness welled up inside her as the fishermen helped her across the gangplank. She couldn't wait to get her feet onto the safety of English soil. She gulped in the air; it was intoxicating. Almost light-headed and still laughing with happiness, she started limping toward the young man, but he was not smiling at her and there was no joy in his waving. Too late she realized he wasn't welcoming her; he was waving her off. Suddenly a car hurtled around the corner and screeched to a stop just inches from her. Two men in black suits jumped out, their fedora hats pulled low over their eyes.

"Hello, we are here to meet you," one said. His voice was clipped, not native English. The other shouted, "We want you to come to work for us." He was closing in on her, his hand reaching into his jacket. Marie-Hélène looked about agitatedly. She saw the young man duck into an alley, and the fishermen aboard the vessel did not look at her as they quickly pushed off from the dock. It was useless to try to run.

She didn't know how long they drove. She dozed off and dreamed of sun-filled days in Calais working in her little bookshop on the main street. She had delighted in the musty smell of the books and enjoyed bantering with her customers. One of them had lured her into the Resistance, and soon she was in charge of recruiting agents and gaining military intelligence which she transmitted to the British War Office. It was beyond exciting, and she planned to write a novel about it all one day.

The wheels crunched on gravel and woke her as the car pulled up in front of an imposing red brick building.

"What's this?" She cried in sudden fright. "Where have you brought me?"

"Oh, it's a hospital," said the clipped voice. "The Home Office will fix your leg and then you'll work for us."

They positioned themselves one each side and half-carried her up the steps. In the entryway there was an elaborate government sign, this hospital was indeed run by the British Home Office, but it wasn't like any hospital she had ever been in. The nurses were dressed more like prison guards. She was mystified to see people slumped in wheelchairs or standing doing nothing, catatonic, heads drooping, mouths drooling. Before she could protest, a nurse slipped a pill into her mouth, and stood over her with a cracked china cup. She gulped the water thirstily; she had had nothing since leaving Calais. Her head immediately started to feel thick, as though it was stuffed with cotton wool. She turned to reach out to the two men who had brought her, but they had vanished. She was told to follow a male nurse, but her body just couldn't muster the strength. He swore impatiently and shoved her into a wheelchair.

At the end of a long bleak corridor, there was a row of showers. Some nurses scrubbed her with lye soap and stiff brushes, re-opening her wounds. The water ran red, and they slapped her to stop her screams. They took a razor to her head. She watched her hair pile up on the dirty floor. She looked about her, her own clothes were gone. They tugged a coarse and shapeless sack dress over her head and wheeled her briskly down a grimy dark corridor. There was an overpowering smell of disinfectant mingled with something like rotting vegetables, only worse. She was rolled into a ward. The beds were packed close together, their white paint chipped down to grey metal. Two harsh lights with green shades dangled on bare cords from the ceiling. The other occupants looked at her blankly, eyes vacant. Some were strapped to their beds, lying in their own filth. She gagged at the stench. The guard indicated a bed, and she fell toward it, her eyelids unbearably heavy. She was unconscious before her head reached the pillow.

The morning brought no relief from the nightmare. The lights had blazed all night, and a nurse, or rather a guard, rushed at her with another pill. She was barely awake, but she had the presence of mind to maneuver it beneath her tongue before she drank the water. She noticed that the totally inert patients in the lobby were ignored. Quickly she adopted their stance, drooping listlessly, mouth agape. It was better that they thought she couldn't walk and couldn't talk.

Her body struggled to heal, but her mind was always active. One day while she was loitering in the lobby, she noticed the reception desk was unmanned, and she drifted toward it, hoping to find a pencil and some paper. She wanted to fill the empty hours secretly writing her story. She noticed *The London Times* lying on the reception desk, and snatched it up, eager for any news. The headlines boasted British military advances. She smiled grimly, it was her resistance unit that had provided crucial military intelligence about German defenses and Wehrmacht deployments, it was she who had planned the acts of sabotage on Nazi telecommunications networks and power grids. British military higher ups had been so grateful for Marie-Hélène's intelligence reports that they sent one of their own wireless operators to assist her. Unfortunately, the wireless operator turned double agent. The Gestapo shot most of her colleagues, and she was arrested and tortured.

The house her unit had operated from was located on the outskirts of Calais. The beating was so horrific and the rape so savage that even the young German guard on duty was revolted. The interrogation had begun peacefully enough. The guard had brought in a wooden chair and placed it in the middle of the room. It was not for her, he motioned her to stay where she was on the concrete floor. A uniformed Gestapo officer came in and sat down on the chair. He removed his leather gloves, and started with small talk, as though he was just there to chat.

He remarked on her broken leg. "Too bad some of the people we hire go too far," he smirked, his pale eyes cold. "But you need to cooperate. Or we'll break the other one." Marie-Hélène said nothing. The officer nodded toward her smashed transmitting equipment and told her she was going to be formally charged as an enemy of the State. He pressed her for information about her comrades and their political activities. Still she said nothing. He raised his voice. She was silent. Her stoic refusal to talk enraged him. He leapt up and barked an order, and a hulking brute lumbered in. He carried a whip of hardened rawhide, its thongs interwoven with wire, the ends hooked and sharpened. The brute stripped off Marie-Hélène's clothes and gripped her by the neck and flung her across the wooden chair. He raised his arm and violently thrashed her bare back and buttocks, grunting with each sickening blow. The Gestapo officer had to shout at the brute to stop him or he would have reduced her to mincemeat. Marie-Hélène collapsed on the floor in her own blood. The Gestapo officer repeated his questions, but she remained silent. Disgusted, he stalked out, slamming the door. The brute threw himself on Marie-Hélène and raped her savagely. He got to his feet, kicked her for good measure and left.

The young guard came in to retrieve the chair. He slipped on the blood and fell hard. He tried to rise, his feet scrabbling to get traction on the sticky floor. He was so unnerved his face was green. He grabbed the chair and ran from the room with it, and Marie-Hélène could hear him vomiting in the hall. She was wracked with pain and could barely breathe, but even in her stupor she was aware that the guard's footsteps were growing fainter. She looked up and realized he had forgotten to close her door. She dragged herself across the room and looked out. The hall was empty save for the bloodied chair. She managed to half crawl half stagger to a window. She wrenched it open and tumbled out.

She heard the squeaking of white hospital shoes approaching, and tossed the newspaper back onto the reception desk, and once again assumed the pose of brain-dead catatonia. The footsteps passed without incident, and taking a deep breath, Marie-Hélène reached for the black phone lying on the desk. She got as far as dialing, but the nurse's squeaking shoes could be heard returning, and Marie-Hélène quietly placed the phone back into its cradle. A woman wearing a black beret sat in a wheelchair across the foyer, silently watching her. Marie-Hélène put a finger to her lips and there was a momentary flash of understanding in the woman's eyes, and then as the nurse strode into view, the woman's head dropped to her chest. Marie-Hélène too assumed the pose. Her head rolled limply to the right, and saliva trickled down her chin.

It was very subtle at first, the nausea and the unexpected headaches. She threw up a few times and she started to have dizzy spells. She had managed to avoid the medications they kept forcing on her, so she knew. Fortunately, the sack dress hid her thickening belly. It was time to formulate a plan. Every day she would wheel herself casually toward the patio doors, pausing frequently to stare blankly into space so as not to attract attention. She would make it outside and sit there for a few minutes and then come back in. One day the woman in the black beret joined her, grinning as though they were naughty schoolgirls playing a prank. The two women sat companionably side by side admiring the gardens.

The woman suddenly glanced behind her and whispered conspiratorially, "My son is coming to get me tomorrow."

Hope leaped in Marie-Hélène's breast, she leaned forward eagerly. "Is he coming in a car? He has a car?"

"Yes," the woman whispered. Her teeth were yellow, rotted. "He's coming in the Rolls Royce with my chauffeur." The woman's eyes glazed over and then she was grinning again at nothing. Marie-Hélène's heart sank.

The next day and the next, Marie-Hélène kept to the same routine. After a breakfast of indescribable mush, she would wheel herself outside. The guards became used to it, they were busy, perpetually short-staffed, and she always looked so innocent, sitting there staring emptily into space. What she was actually gazing at was the wall. She was trying to gauge the distance and look for gaps. One day when she was rolling toward the door, she spotted a hat and coat on the pegs in the entry, temporarily left there by a visitor. Marie-Hélène quickly snatched them and bundled them onto her wheelchair and sat down on top. She rolled toward the patio. It seemed quiet; the guards were busy elsewhere. She rolled a little further away from the door, watching, listening. Nobody came. She went a bit further and was about to make her big move, when she heard a voice calling her. It was the woman in the black beret, wheeling herself out onto the patio. Marie-Hélène hesitated, weighing the situation, and then decided to make a run for it anyway.

Just then a guard burst through the door and ran toward Marie-Hélène. The woman in the beret leaped up, and with a rock she had hidden in her lap, she bashed in the back of the guard's head. He dropped to the ground and lay still. The woman blew her a kiss, and Marie-Hélène whisked off the sack dress, pulled on the hat and coat, and headed for the boundary wall. Stumbling across bumpy grass, she sought the spot where she could shimmy through.

The hat hid her bald head, and the voluminous coat covered her figure and she blended in with the passersby. She stood on a street corner wondering what to do next, when somebody handed her a coin, thinking she was begging. She stepped into the red telephone booth and used it to dial. She reached her contact in one try. She waited on the corner and soon he came to pick her up. The Bobbies turned a blind eye, just another john.

"I tried to warn you off at the dock," he said.

"I know you did. More important, you've got a mole."

"We know who it is. We'll pick him up when you're safely out of the country, so there's no reprisals."

He drove her to the coast and got her onto a fishing trawler bound for Calais. She was eight months pregnant when she rejoined the Resistance. Her story would have a few more chapters.

GETTING THE STORY

He had the kind of nervous energy that just couldn't spend days cooped up at a desk, so he eagerly took all the assignments where he'd have to go out and find the story himself. And this one was a doozy. Winston was hanging around the police station when they came in, the German woman and her daughter.

The mother was dressed like someone out of a 1940s movie. Her hair was carefully rolled up into a pompadour high on her forehead and secured with bobby pins. A black pill-box hat clung precariously to the back of her head. She wore a tailored black suit jacket with wide mutton-leg sleeves and a fluttering peplum that exaggerated her hips. A large glittering brooch hugged her lapel at a jaunty angle. She wore black gloves and carried a black handbag on her arm, and she teetered into the room on sky-high black pumps. Clark Gable would have leaned out of the silver screen and given her a thumbs up.

She told them her name was Greta.

"Oh, Greta Garbo." The detective was gently teasing her, making a little joke, but all the policemen were struggling to keep straight faces. Winston sidled into the room, notebook at the ready, prepared to do his thing as a journalist and get the story.

Ten years in England had not unclogged the woman's accent. "You should know I *could* have been a movie star. I was the most beautiful girl in my village," she told the detective. Her voice was throaty, guttural.

The men stifled their laughter, but their mouths twitched. The detective eased his ample thigh onto the front of his desk and shifted his weight until he was comfortable. He planted one foot firmly on the floor, swinging the other. He had a sheet of paper in his hand. He said directly to the child, "Do you mind if I ask you some questions?" The little girl squirmed on the hard chair. Her feet dangled and the edge of the wooden seat cut into the backs of her legs.

The mother adjusted her gloves. "Of course, you can ask me anything you want, that is why I am here."

The detective ignored her and leaned closer to the child. "You walked to school that day, right past the factory. Did you notice anyone there?" Before the child could answer, her mother had opened a compact and powdered her nose and then popped the top off a tube of bright red lipstick, and leaning in close to the mirror, applied it thickly, compressing her lips to set it. And then she posed with one hand seductively next to her cheek. Somebody in the room snickered. Winston knew he should maintain a journalist's impartial composure, but he couldn't help whispering to the nearest police officer, "Doesn't she know this is a murder investigation and not an audition for a part in a movie?"

The child amused herself rocking her legs back and forth in time with the inspector's swinging foot. The mother didn't encourage the child to answer any questions. Instead, she fussed with her hair and picked invisible lint off her skirt.

"I am trying to remember if my daughter even went to school that day. Maybe she didn't."

"Yes, Ma'am, she did. She was late, but the school did sign her in." The detective's voice was weary.

Winston whispered to the uniform next to him, "I bet the kid knows a whole lot more than she's letting on. If you could get the kid away from the mother, you might learn something."

The policeman whispered back, "The mother's loopy and the kid's too young. A waste of time, I'd say."

The woman was still trying to hog center stage. She spread bright red lips showing her teeth in a glamorous smile and tilted her head charmingly.

"All the boys wanted to marry me. But I left them all behind and married a handsome English army officer." She smiled coquettishly.

"War bride?" Winston whispered. The uniform next to him nodded yes, "But he left her."

The policemen standing around had been amused at first, but eventually they grew tired of straining to understand Greta's accent and watching her affected mannerisms. They drifted out of the room. The detective slid off his desk. He had other things to do.

"Well, if you do remember anything ..." he said, and waited for them to stand up.

The child jumped down from the chair. The detective patted her shoulder, and Winston went over and gave her a little bag of sweets. He smiled warmly. "You did a very good job," he told her.

Winston sneaked a look at the police log and saw that they lived on Churchill Close. He parked and walked round there the next afternoon. It was a tightly packed circle of red brick low-income council houses. He located the small flat where Greta lived. He was so engrossed in studying the building that he stepped right into the path of a teenager riding his bicycle on the walkway.

"Watch it! You a copper?"

"Is it that obvious?" Winston brushed himself off, unashamed of lying to get his story.

"The police have already been sniffing around. They talked to all the neighbors. So, what's it worth?" Winston dug in his pocket and handed over a few coins.

"Well, the murdered man lived there in that building." Winston's eyes widened, the flat the boy was pointing to was right opposite Greta's. "Frankie never really had a job. He was nearly thirty, but he lived with his sister and her family. Mostly sat chain-smoking in his underwear in the alleyway between the two buildings. That's his neighbor, Greta and her kid coming home now." A woman and child were walking toward them carrying shopping bags. Winston didn't recognize them at first because the mother was dressed perfectly normally in a plain brown wool coat, matching headscarf and sensible walking shoes. Winston hastily thanked the youth, and hiding his face in his collar, he hurried around the corner to his car.

From there he drove over to take a look at the factory. Winston knew the road the detective had been talking about. The factory was an abandoned concrete shell, crumbling, filled with rubble, and the lane that had served it was now a little-used shortcut to the village. Most people preferred to go the long way round. Winston thought how brave of the child to walk to school through that sinister tunnel of trees.

He knew he shouldn't, but he did. The next morning, he waited for the child. She recognized him from the police station and smiled. Winston walked along with her, and she seemed glad to have the company. He chatted a bit about her school, and then he got to the point. "Frankie lived near you?"

"Yes. He's dead now." She was splashing her Wellington boots in overflowing potholes.

"Did you know him very well?"

"He lived right opposite our front door, and he watched me all the time. He called me Kraut Kid, and always yelled at me," she mimicked his sing-song voice, "you lost the war, you lost the war."

Winston sidestepped a puddle to preserve his good shoes. "That was very mean of him. Do you know what happened to him that day at the factory?"

"Well, he kind of jumped out at me and said he wanted to be friends, and that he had someone he wanted me to meet inside the factory."

Winston's hackles rose, a cold shiver ran down his back. He asked quietly, "Did you go in there with him?"

"I didn't want to but he got ahold of my arm."

Winston was almost afraid to ask the next question. "What happened then?"

The child hesitated, as though unwilling to relive an unpleasant memory. "Well, there's no people in there anymore, but he pulled me inside. I was scared and screamed so he pushed me on the ground. Then my mother came up behind him and suddenly he fell down. She had a big piece of iron pipe in her hand. She said to me, I ran after you with your lunch. She said here take your lunch, go quickly to school or you'll be late."

They walked in silence. Winston finally said, "She pretended to be a crazy lady so the police wouldn't ask you too many questions, didn't she."

The child giggled. "She said she was playing dressing up. Didn't she look pretty?"

"Yes, she did. Listen to me now, it's very important. Don't you ever tell anyone what you told me today, OK?"

"Ok," she said.

"Cross your heart?"

"Cross my heart."

Winston walked with her to the school steps and stood waving until she disappeared inside. He already knew this was a story he was never going to write.

AS SIMPLE AS THAT

I'm cold," the child whined.

His mother jiggled him in her arms, "How can you be cold, we're in tropical Australia," she joked.

"We're all cold," said a man. "They must have scrubbed all the bloody paint off it by now."

Someone else in the crowd said, "I could have *walked* to Sydney in the time we've been in this bloody hangar." Everybody laughed.

The child continued to whine. "But why are we here? Why aren't we on the plane?"

His mother said, "Because there's insects on the plane they don't want in Australia. All international flights have to get washed. Here, Bobby," she set him down. "Here's your coloring book and your box of crayons. Why don't you just kneel down here and do some coloring? Hmmm?"

"I don't wanna color ..." Bobby's voice was drowned out by a sudden commotion at the plane.

"It's stowaways, they found stowaways!"

The news rippled through the crowd. Everybody rushed to the open door of the hangar and peered into the darkness.

"How many were there?"

"Quite a bunch, apparently. They're taking them to a hotel."

"A hotel? Wait, hold on just one bloody minute. The paying passengers are standing in a freezing cold concrete hangar, and the stowaways are being taken to a *hotel*?"

"That's what the customs guy said. They thought they were in America. They got on the wrong plane."

"So they couldn't even get *that* right? Look, they're coming out now."

Everybody raised up on tiptoe and stretched their necks. The stowaways were herded into a single file by the officers and marched across the tarmac.

"They're a pretty ratty mob. And there's kids."

Bobby looked up. "Kids?" His mother wasn't listening. Bobby pushed aside his coloring book and elbowed his way through the forest of legs.

A man said, "Well, I hope they're put on the next flight to America. I'll even chip in to pay for it." Laughter.

"Look, they're coming through the door now." They all craned to see. "Go back where you came from," someone muttered. People around him murmured in agreement.

Bobby reached out and handed a passing kid a red crayon. The child stopped and looked at it in wonder. He turned it over in his hands, he traced the contours with a grimy finger, and he tried it out on the palm of his hand and held it up for Bobby to see. Smiling, he ran to catch up with his parents. A hush fell on the watching crowd. Into the silence blared a raucous overhead announcement.

"Passengers continuing on to Sydney and Melbourne please re-board your aircraft."

People hoisted their belongings and shuffled forward. "I got a lawn to mow, ha-ha, I coulda actually stayed a bit longer."

"Me too. I know the wife's got a Honey-Do list a mile long waiting for me." They jostled each other good-naturedly as they climbed back on the plane.

MEMOIRS OF A JUNK YARD DOG

Rottweiler puppies must be the cutest on earth. And they can fetch quite a price from upstanding ethical breeders who monitor the blood lines and get regular health certifications. But Guppy wasn't one of those Rottweilers. He came from a puppy mill, and his price, even if he had looked healthy, would have been half that rate. But he didn't look healthy, he had hip dysplasia and crooked knees. As a result, one dark night the puppy mill owners took a ride, and speeding down the freeway, tossed Guppy out of the car window.

The Boss and Mrs. Boss spotted him the next day, cowering, shivering and terrified, between the median guard rails. The Boss screeched to a halt and backed up, a dangerous thing to do on a busy freeway, but he did it, and Mrs. Boss jumped out and snatched up Guppy and cradled him in her arms all the way home.

Guppy had thick glossy black fur and handsome tan markings on his snout and paws. His eyes were warm brown puddles that gazed gratefully and lovingly at Mrs. Boss from the minute she picked him up. But his jaw had been dislocated in the fall, giving him a permanent snarl. The Boss laughed when he saw the snarl and declared: "How perfect is that for a junk yard dog!"

Guppy settled in. He slept in a 1970s Mustang which had been stripped of parts but kept its seats, and he had lots of room to roam. His job was to protect The Boss' junkyard which was surrounded by a chain link fence. Guppy was uncertain whether the fence was to keep him in, or unwanted visitors out. It served neither purpose, since teenagers had long ago clipped a hole in the chain-link in one far corner, and they came and went as they pleased. Guppy could have left at any time, but why would he? He had a comfy bed, regular meals, and peaceful days.

It wasn't that he was lazy, no, not at all. He kept up his thrice daily patrols, briskly trotting the perimeter in rain or blistering heat. Each morning he arose and headed for the first point of his patrol next to a lipstick pink azalea, from which he could see Mrs. Boss at her kitchen window, feeding the fish. He figured that was where his name came from. His damaged jaw never did close properly, and it clacked loosely when he ate, so he looked a lot like one of Mrs. Boss' guppies when feeding. From the azalea he headed out on a well-worn path around the edge of the chain-link. On sunny days he would linger, gazing at the butterflies and birds. He would pass the hole in the fence with barely a glance. The teenage boys who occasionally sneaked in were harmless and Guppy never minded them. They climbed into the vintage cars, and pretended they were zooming round the Indy 500 track. Guppy could watch them from his Mustang bed, pleased to have the company, and enjoying the break in the monotony.

He rarely saw The Boss. The Boss was beefy tattooed ex-Navy, and like many who went bald on top, he carefully nurtured a fringe of long white hair beginning just above his ears and cascading down to his shoulders. He headed out early every morning, returning only to back his truck through the gate to drop off some scrap, tow in a rusted jalopy, or to meet and make a deal with the occasional buyer. On those occasions Guppy kept a respectful distance, hovering just close enough to demonstrate a menacing security presence, his crooked jaw exposing dangerous jagged teeth, fearsome enough to freeze one's blood.

One morning on his patrol, Guppy was surprised that Mrs. Boss was not at the window feeding her fish. Guppy could see that they were swarming in anxious circles near the top of the tank. He watched for a few minutes, but he had places to go and things to do, and so he continued on his patrol. When he had completed the circuit, instead of going back to his Mustang bed as he usually did, a nagging concern propelled him once more to the azalea, and he scanned the kitchen window. The fish were clearly alarmed, and Mrs. Boss was nowhere in sight.

So, Guppy took matters in hand. He went to the hole in the fence, squeezed through, left the junkyard, and trotted round the outside perimeter over to the house. He jumped up on the front step and gave a quick bark. Nothing. He barked twice, not too loudly, but just to let Mrs. Boss know he was there. He heard a faint cry. He hastened to the kitchen window, not the one with the fish tank, but the open one next to it, and put his front paws up on the sill, peering inside. Mrs. Boss was lying on the floor. Guppy did not waste a second. He hurled himself through the window and raced to her side. She was weak but was able to raise her head slightly.

"Oh, Guppy," she said. "The phone, get the phone." She was pointing to the kitchen counter.

Now Rottweilers are well known for their patience, their protectiveness, and their loyalty, but what many people don't know is that they are also extremely intelligent. Guppy could see that Mrs. Boss wanted something from the kitchen counter, so with one bound, he sprang up, and began hurling everything that was on the counter to the floor. Flour bin, cookie jar, the electric mixer, a rolling pin, the sugar bowl, a book of recipes, one after the other they all clattered to the floor. The final item to hit the floor was Mrs. Boss' cell phone.

He could see that was the thing that pleased her the most, so he nudged the cell phone toward her until she was able to grasp it in her hand. With trembling fingers, she punched in 911.

Guppy lay down by Mrs. Boss, and she put her hand on his back. Reassured by his presence, she calmed immediately, and together they waited until help came.

THE NEST

Kylie eyed her father sitting comfortably across the table, nose deep in his newspaper. She searched her mind for a topic.

"Look what the poets said about suffering," she said, with an air of seriousness that she hoped would get his attention. She held out a book from school. Her father wasn't interested in poets, and he didn't ask her whether she was suffering.

"Oh, I'm sure they all suffered," was all he said. He pointedly rustled his newspaper. Kylie didn't care. It was not so much that she wanted to discuss poetry anyway, it was more to show the woman that they were a twosome, she and her father, and that the woman was not part of it. But her father was not performing as Kylie hoped.

The woman was quietly setting the table for breakfast. Kylie got up and came around to lean against her father's arm. He continued reading. Sighing, she went back to her seat at the table. The woman placed a fork on the table. Kylie immediately moved it an inch to the left.

"It's windy, I can't go out," she said to her father. He was still hidden behind his paper. Getting no response, she glanced out the window. Gnarled grey trees crouched low, their grotesque shapes in stark contrast against the looming prescient sky. New green shoots tossed this way and that in helpless fluttering chaos, and somewhere an unlatched gate clattered. It was the time of uncertainty between winter and spring. Winter was reluctant to let go.

"The baby birds will fall out of their nests in this wind," Kylie said.

"They won't fall far," her father said absently. Kylie got up and walked around the table again and leaned over his shoulder. He patted her arm and continued reading. She put her arms around his chest, her cheek next to his. He didn't put down his paper, so she started to smother his cheek with wet little kisses, the way she had when she was a small child. It had always delighted him then and had made him laugh. But now he dodged his head away, one eye still on his newspaper. Kylie hung on the side of his chair for a few minutes, then she tried to wedge into the small space between him and the table.

"You're too big for my lap," her father said, gently nudging her aside.

Kylie noisily threw herself onto her own chair and took out her cell phone.

"Where's Winnie." She said it irritably, hearing the woman clatter plates in the kitchen. She was not expecting an answer. When the woman first came to live with them, Kylie's father had explained to her that the name Winyan is Lakota Sioux for "mature woman." Kylie had put her fingers in her ears when he said that, and she had always persisted in referring to the woman as Winnie. Her father had mistaken it for an Anglicized term of endearment, and he was satisfied, but Kylie hoped the woman noticed the real intention behind the snarky condescending and belittling diminutive.

She looked for ways to provoke her. Just that morning Kylie had tried on outfit after outfit, and unable to choose, had flung them all to the floor in disgust. The woman patiently picked them up, ironed them, and hung them back in her closet. Kylie had sneaked in and thrown them all on the floor again. The woman hadn't seen that yet. Kylie smiled grimly to herself.

Annoyingly, the woman had always seemed unaware of Kylie's objective. She went about her daily tasks, her serene face implacable, brown eyes tranquil, unperturbed. She glided silently from room to room, radiating immutable strength and stability. She filled the dark corners with light, she brought life to each barren space, she brought warmth where there had been none. Kylie's father had started to smile again.

Just a faint whoosh of her skirts announced the woman's return from the kitchen. Kylie looked with exaggerated disdain at the woman's clothes, woven in the muted shades of the distant mountains, and pointedly smoothed and rearranged her own citrus green shirt and neon yellow skirt. She was showing the woman *this* is how *we* dress.

The woman put a plate of avocado toast in front of Kylie. Kylie ignored it, and instead, leaned over to show her father a picture on her cell phone, angling it so that only he could see it, deliberately excluding the woman. He nodded absently.

Only when the woman had left the room did Kylie pull the plate toward her. The toast was exactly the right golden brown, piled with exactly the right amount of avocado, and Kylie ate it with relish. She kept an eye on the door lest the woman catch her enjoying it. Her father was deep in his world news, unaware of the drama playing out around him in his own home.

The woman came back into the room. Her hair rippled to her waist like a shimmering river in the storm's vibrant light. She set down a plate of bacon and eggs. Kylie's father looked up at her, his face breaking into a smile, aglow with gratitude, acknowledging that this woman could embrace two lost souls, and raise his child as her own. There passed between them a look of deep affection. Kylie recoiled in shock, as though a sharp knife had pierced her belly. Her anger rose like acid in her throat. She looked from one to the other in fury. But when she looked into Winyan's eyes, instead of the triumph Kylie expected to see there, those eyes held nothing but kindness.

Kylie slumped back in her chair and slid down low. She realized with dismay that though she had clung to the grief, the hurt, the loss that had been their bond, her father had moved on to a place she could not yet follow. A pang of longing surprised her, and for a moment she couldn't speak.

She said finally, a catch in her voice, "Oh look, there's the sun. I can go out after all."

She wanted to be alone, to cry for the past, for the future, for the pain of change, for all these things, and most of all for another woman's selfless guidance that was showing her the way to leave the world of childhood.

DON'T FORGET TO PAY THE LADY

In the early morning, those deep concrete canyons are morbidly dank and cold. The fog is a dirty yellow gritty miasma filling each trough. The surrounding windows are dark like blind eyes, gazing at nothing, seeing nothing. Rain-slick streets welcome no-one, their fetid gutters only there to dump and carry away stale hopes and still-born dreams into bottomless holes.

One such hole was approached by two women lugging between them a rolled-up carpet. The two bent together and lifted the iron manhole cover. They upended the carpet, and its contents slid smoothly into the black hole. They replaced the manhole cover, and hurried away, taking the carpet with them.

✝ ✝ ✝

I could see two pairs of glinting eyes and hear the scratching of their claws, and feel them near me, waiting, just waiting. I lay there naked and bruised from the fall. I wanted to cover and protect my private parts, but I couldn't move. Cold sewage pooled around me, the acrid stench clogging my nostrils, searing my lungs and stinging my eyeballs. Eventually the coldness of the sludge revived me. To my surprise one of my hands started to twitch, then I was able to move one foot, and then the other. Whatever it was the women had given me was starting to wear off. Cautiously I tried out different parts of my body, and eventually managed, after three tries, to sit up. I heard the little squeaks of disappointment at losing a taste of flesh, and that galvanized me to crawl away from those creatures, heaving myself across a pile of slime as gross and impenetrable as a carbuncle. I felt along the wall for the iron step ladder and grasped the lowest rung. Slowly, hand-over-hand I hauled myself up, painfully clawing from one rung to the next, groping ever upward. Heartened by my progress I found the strength to make it to the top, where my head butted the ceiling of my tomb. I strained and strained but could not move the round iron lid. I felt hot tears on my cheeks. I had planned to buy bar bells and work out, and I vowed if I made it, I would join a gym. Finally, using my shoulders, I heaved with all my might and managed to raise the manhole cover. I stood there on the top run, my head finally above ground breathing in the air and luxuriating in the cool mist falling gently on my face, and I laughed out loud.

✦ ✦ ✦

She had been wearing a red lacey bra, I could see her nipples through the mesh, and I felt the perspiration course down my temples. It was just like the one I had bought at Victoria's Secret for my wife. She had never worn it for me, of course. Probably wore it for that scum she ran off with. Well, too bad she can't see me now with this gorgeous woman. Maybe I should give her a call and mention casually that I had someone new, someone beautiful, and someone who wanted to be with me.

The drink was strong, one sip was enough, and when my hostess left the room, I poured it into the fishbowl. I thought back to our meeting. It was one of those instant connections, I suppose. This gorgeous woman spotted me across the room. She came over to me in the coffee shop and out of the blue, asked me out for a drink. We only made it to a bar, then she suggested we immediately come up to her place. It did occur to me in a passing wisp of clarity that she might be a hooker. The chance meeting was, even to me, a bit unlikely. But I suppose I was thrilled, flattered and grinning foolishly, thoroughly besotted with the woman, aware that I should maybe have found out how much this evening was going to cost me, but knowing I was never going to ask. After all, I have looked in the mirror. I did color my hair, and I did buy a couple of new suits when my wife left, but that didn't do me any good. My wife left me two years ago, and nobody else had filled the lonely void.

Until now.

When I glanced back at the fishbowl, the goldfish was floating belly up on the surface.

They were sitting on a couch across the room from me. I could hear them talking, they didn't even keep their voices low, as though they took it for granted that I couldn't hear them. I don't know where the other woman came from. She had appeared suddenly. Her voice sounded familiar, the accent, could it be, yeah, I think it was, it was one of my employees, it was my marketing director. I tried to raise my eyelids, but they were unbearably heavy, and I could only make out vague blurry images. My arms and legs were numb, immobile. I flashed on the thought that if I had drained my glass, I would probably be belly-up like that goldfish over there.

"It was an ambush," my marketing director was telling the other woman. "I walked into the conference room and there was the accountant and the sales manager sitting at that long table with old Dim Dickhead."

Tim *Dirkhead*, I shouted in my mind. No sound came out, my lips weren't moving, they seemed frozen, but I was thinking it loudly in my mind, how could she get my name wrong, she works right there in my office.

"That hair-ball of a sales manager Andy said I hadn't given him the set-up costs. I mean he makes an $80,000 mistake and says it was my fault because I didn't give him the set up costs? I said Oh but I did, and I also told him that if people don't want to buy one of that author's paperbacks for 99 cents, they aren't going to buy ten of that author's paperbacks in a set for $99. That was a huge mistake for a small publishing company, but you know what Dickhead said? He said Oh, you didn't make the costs clear to Andy."

I tried to raise my head. I wanted to say but Andy is my only friend, he's been my sales manager for years, of course I had to defend him. But they kept on talking, those two sitting close together, sharing secrets like old friends do, plotting and planning. Try as I might, my voice stayed inside my head. I knew they couldn't hear me.

My marketing director was saying resentfully, "I didn't get my raise. Old Boys' Club, glass ceiling stuff."

The women stood up. "Well, let's get on with it."

I thought oh good, my marketing director is letting bygones be bygones. I'd maybe even consider giving her that raise when we got back to the office. Not an apology, you can't admit you were wrong and maybe Andy did lie, yes, I'm pretty sure he did, but maybe I can manage the raise.

The women shrugged into their tan trench-coats and buttoned up. Which was odd, because then they started to *undress* me. They pulled off my shirt, unbuckled my belt and tipped me over to tug off my pants. I giggled inside my head, aware that though I would love to assist, in my awkward stupor I was in no condition to do so. But I was thinking, Yes! The party is about to begin. I feared my equipment might be as useless as my tongue, but I was nevertheless eager to see what they had in mind.

One grasped my feet, the other took my arms, and they frog-marched me over to the front door. To my surprise they rolled me into the entry-way carpet. It was a very nice one, a red oriental I had actually admired on the way in, and now they were rolling me into it. I noticed that my pasty white stomach stood out in stark contrast to the rich crimson wool. I hoped the women didn't notice.

I giggled inside my head again as they lifted me and carried me away. All part of the fun and games I suppose.

✝ ✝ ✝

There was a light rain falling, a wall of heavy mist really, you could see it bouncing the headlights back into the driver's face. You know how it is when you have to be up in the wee small hours to start work, and you really aren't too alert, you are operating on automatic? When you are trundling down a dark New York street at 3 AM to make an early delivery, it's not likely, well, you just wouldn't expect to see a head suddenly pop up out of a manhole, would you. There was a slight thud, then a squish, something like running over a ripe watermelon. It had to be several seconds before the driver even realized.

You wouldn't stop, why would you. You would do what he did, you would keep going, and you would do what he did, deliberately driving into every overflowing pothole to wash off anything that might be sticking to your tires.

A CHILL WIND

It felt like a mercy date to him, but he pushed aside the thought, hopeful still to retrieve whatever there had been. He tried a lawyer joke to keep her attention.

"Why do old lawyers never die?" He thought the joke would amuse her and that she would smile indulgently, impressed that he was poking fun at himself. Then her lips would part, he would see the pink tongue, the small perfectly set white teeth, and she would smile up at him, and he would know everything was alright.

He silently congratulated himself, the joke was a calculated move, he thought he had made his case well, and that she would see that he was not pretending to be her contemporary, as so many middle-aged men tend to do. He wanted her to understand that though they were officially professor/student, there was more between them that could and would outlast the lecture hall.

He waited, holding his breath, for her verdict.

Her eyes flicked briefly to his face, and away. She didn't bother to speak. His splinter of hope was starting to wither.

"They just appeal!" he said gamely.

There was a pause. "They have their habeas corpus," she murmured absently. It was almost too much effort for her to say the words.

His eyebrows shot up, his face flushed, he was excited that she had responded to him, and so cleverly too.

A breeze came up, and a strand of her hair lifted and veiled her cheek. She turned her head slightly to let the next gust blow it back into place. Her lashes were the same wheat color as her hair, and rimmed translucent eyes that reflected the pearl-grey sky.

Brittle leaves crunched under his shoes as he moved in front of her, trying to put himself within the range of her gaze. He slid his hand into his pocket, fingers curling around the envelope there.

But alas, she looked right through him, out, and away to a landscape as bleak as he suddenly felt. She might as well have looked at her watch or checked her cell phone.

He took his hand out of his pocket, empty.

He knew then that there would be no lively sunshine-filled trip to Hawaii, his hope now as cold as the wind that heralded the coming winter.

THE INCORRIGIBLE HERO

So, Cecil, your play is opening tomorrow?"

"Yes. I am the star." Cecil glanced around trying to figure out which camera was focused on him.

"That's wonderful. Break a leg. My note here says you're pretty new at acting." Cecil didn't know he was supposed to respond. He was still looking for the camera. "It's the one with the red light, Cecil," said the interviewer. "What did you do before you became an actor, Cecil?"

Cecil rearranged his features to portray a sad victim.

"I was laid off because of COVID from my high-level executive position at a big bank in the city, you know, the big black marble one."

"Oh? Which bank is that again?" The interviewer made a note on her clipboard.

Cecil was seized by an uncontrollable and loud fit of coughing. It was so severe that he was rendered speechless. A go-fer ran to him with a glass of water. Cecil took a sip and made use of the lull in the conversation to wave at the cameraman, the cameraman's assistant, the makeup lady, and a passing electrician.

The interviewer felt it would be alright to resume the interview. "So, you were a high-level bank executive …?" Cecil's cough immediately became much worse, and he fluttered his hands to show he could not go on.

"Well, OK," the interviewer said, looking at her notes. She crossed her legs. "Let's see, let's try another one. 2021 has been a difficult, if not a tragic, year for a lot of us. COVID, layoffs, shutdowns. What would be your wish for next year, 2022?"

Cecil's cough magically disappeared, and he put his finger on his chin, giving the question a lot of thought.

"Well," he said slowly, "I would wish that I don't just continue as a star of the stage, I want very much to be on television ..."

His publicist hastily whispered something. Cecil looked irritated, but added, "And world peace."

The interviewer was ready to present her next question, but Cecil had turned away and was leaning toward the camera. He was trying to angle his head so that the camera pointed to his left side, which wasn't easy since the camera was to his right. Cecil believed his left side was his best. His head was twisted awkwardly, but he overcame that discomfort with determination. He tried for an intense Valentino smolder directly into the lens.

Out of camera range, the interviewer spread her hands helplessly. The publicist waved her arms, trying to refocus Cecil's attention, but to no avail. The camera was moving in, and Cecil was inching forward to meet it, until finally the lens was tightly concentrated on his left nostril. The publicist frantically circled an index finger, signaling the interviewer to wrap it up.

The interviewer said, "Well, thank you for taking the time to be with us ..."

Cecil stretched his mouth to get every last dazzling tooth into the frame, and without moving his lips he mumbled, "What channel will this be shown on?"

His publicist hissed, "Say it's been a pleasure ..."

But Cecil and the camera were locked together in their symbiotic dance, each unwilling to break the spell. All

Cecil could manage through clenched teeth was, "Could I get a copy of this video for my portfolio?"

The play closed in two nights. The last night's performance was actually courtesy of the director's father, he had bought all the tickets, paid a couple of reviewers to show up, and seated some homeless folk in the front three rows. Next day Cecil was thrilled to see his name in print. He had to search, the reviews appeared in a couple of the more minor trades, but he found them.

The first one was in the bottom third of page 8, between service ads offering dog-walking and tarot card readings.

> **"A study in shameless hokum, the production struggles to maintain any momentum, with uninteresting characters and implausible scenes. The herky-jerky studied mannerisms of the star Cecil caused the only amusement, and his inaudible delivery provided welcome relief from listening to the atrocious dialogue. For this we came out of lockdown?"**

In the second publication, the review was on page 12, below the legals and next to an illustrated ad for an escort service.

> **"The production was insufferably preachy and infuriatingly manipulative, and the audience experienced nothing but wretched confusion. It was noise without meaning, action without thrills, violence without cause, comedy without laughs. Cecil, the inept star, provided a devastating death-knell to this cringe-worthy schmaltz. I would humbly beg that we can all go back into lockdown."**

Cecil cut out both articles, and carefully pasted them into his scrapbook where he had already placed three of his professional photos.

If you just glanced quickly at his photos, you could be impressed. He had large brown eyes and a small nose. Out of the frame was a burgeoning 44-year-old belly and a couple of bad knees. Also, it should be noted that no middle-aged man could still have such a chiclet-bright perfectly matched set of white teeth. For the truly picky, one eyebrow arched much higher than the other giving his face a perpetually bewildered air, and a button nose does not necessarily become a grown man, and to the obnoxiously persnickety observer, an asymmetrical face such as Cecil's looks like it was spitefully assembled by Picasso.

Be that as it may, Cecil's self-importance had all the enthusiasm of a man enjoying huge success. Walking down the street, any random honking horn caused him to whirl, teeth ablaze, arm raised to greet his fans. That the honking horn was at a distant intersection did not diminish the bounce in Cecil's swagger. That is not to say that Cecil did not have fans. His childhood friend Brogan was steadfast and loyal. Though Brogan currently hawked questionably branded leather goods from a hole-in-the-wall alley in the Bronx, he had his own aspirations of becoming an actor. Knowing a Broadway star like Cecil certainly added to his street cred, and he was agog with the potential of Cecil's useful connections. That Cecil's play was off, off, off, Broadway didn't matter, just the word Broadway was sufficient to ensure Brogan's devoted awe. It was unlikely that he would ever see the reviews in the New York trades, or know that the play had closed, and Cecil saw no reason to share that information with him. Or to introduce him to his live-in love, who might have unintentionally spilled the beans. That was Cassandra Louise, his erstwhile playwright/director, and daughter of the generous father who had kept her show, and his stardom, afloat for that one extra day.

Cecil's publicist was long gone, in fact she had disappeared immediately after the interview. She didn't even wait to collect her fee. Absent any more planned Cassandra Louise writing/directorial efforts, Cecil did make some lack-luster rounds of actor's agencies, but only because someone had told him that's what actors do. He made it very clear to the agency reps that he was only available short-term, that he was on-call by a top director, and that he found the whole audition thing a bore. Since he didn't have the fee for their services, and demonstrated no discernible talent, personality or connections, the meetings always ended abruptly. But Cecil already had all he needed. Cassandra Louise's father was footing their household bills so Cecil could pretend to his friends in the Outer Boroughs that he continued to be wildly successful at his new craft. The admiration that was as necessary to him as oxygen came with the veneration of Brogan, and all his old pals in the 'hood, for his presumed stratospheric stardom. Overall, it was a very desirable state of equilibrium for Cecil, and one which Cecil could have, and would have, continued indefinitely.

Thus, Cecil was totally surprised and rudely bounced out of his fantasy one day, by Cassandra Louise casually mentioning that she was thinking of moving on. She had always been quiet, compliant, agreeable, so this came out of the blue. Eventually, Cecil had assumed, Cassandra Louise would star him in another of her father-funded plays. It was unforeseen, unexpected, and utterly unimagined by Cecil that beneath Cassandra Louise's tranquil countenance there simmered ambitions that she felt could not be furthered by her association with him. Also, her father had suddenly pulled the plug on the cash-flow.

Delusions as stalwart as Cecil's creep up like ivy latching onto a wall, even to the point where the wall itself is supported solely by the smothering parasite. There is nothing so compelling as the stories we tell ourselves. Thus, still infused with the heady aura of his own fictional accomplishments, Cecil travelled to the Outer Burroughs to devise a cunning plan. He wanted to prevent the collapse of his comfortable world, and he saw the unwitting Brogan as a useful accomplice in his scheme. He met with his faithful friend and explained to Brogan that if he, Brogan, would execute a certain deed, sort of like an acting rehearsal if you will, then Brogan could, if he performed well, expect to have a part in one of Cecil's eventual Broadway plays.

Late one night, after enjoying one of the TV couch-and-desk talk shows Cecil loved to watch – he imagined himself exchanging witty bon mots with the hosts – Cecil and Cassandra Louise prepared for bed. Cecil brought two cups of steaming hot chocolate to the bedroom. Cassandra Louise, surprised at Cecil's unusual gesture, appreciatively drank hers, and promptly fell into a very deep sleep. Sometime later, she awoke to the horror of a knee on her chest and a hand clamped over her nose and mouth. She was nothing if not resourceful, so she bit down hard on the hand of her attacker, who dived headfirst out through a window that was conveniently left wide open.

Cecil, who for some reason was not in the bed with her at the time, lingered a moment outside the door, then responded to Cassandra Louise's screams by bounding dramatically into the room with loud unintelligible exclamations. Rather than inquiring what had happened, Cecil explained at length to Cassandra Louise his reasons for being out of their bed and in the kitchen at 3 AM.

Cassandra Louise was reluctant, due to shyness or shock, to say very much at all, other than that the attacker's hand had smelled strongly of leather. Cecil was happy to take over the interviews. The press was eager to hear the details, and Cecil did not disappoint. He grandly recounted how he had rushed to Cassandra Louise's rescue in the terrifying home invasion and managed to chase away the attacker. He honed and perfected the story which grew exponentially with each telling. He took great care that the cameras caught his good side, and he always provided journalists with copies of his headshot. "You will probably need some photos to use in your story …" he told them.

Cassandra Louise's father was unfortunately not as impressed by Cecil's heroism as Cecil had hoped, and he packed up her belongings and took her away. In the absence of any other photos being provided by the family, Cecil's headshot appeared on television and in the newspapers. Cecil's publicist immediately saw a reason to return his calls. She invited Cecil to bunk on her couch and arranged for him to guest on a late show. Well, a late, late, late, show.

Cecil told the late-night host an enhanced and richly embroidered version of how he was able to save Cassandra Louise's life by fighting off the heavily armed attacker. Brogan, who was in the audience and still nursing his heavily bandaged hand, laughed so loudly that he was almost ejected from the studio. But the studio audience and the viewing public were captivated by the unflinching bravery of this up-and-coming actor. Cecil was offered a small, one line role in an off-Broadway play. Well, an off, off, off, Broadway play.

In the audience on opening night, which was unfortunately also closing night, sat Cecil's faithful childhood friend, the aspiring actor Brogan. Brogan had shut down his Bronx leather goods enterprise and moved to the City, encouraged and more eager than ever to launch his show-biz career, considering his acting experience in Cassandra Louise's bedroom. Cecil's promises offered the pathway to his lifelong dream of stardom, and there he sat, front row center, dotingly watching his mentor.

It was probably around the middle of the first act, when the audience was growing restive at the uninspiring proceedings, when Cecil paused in the middle of his one line. He raised one hand dramatically and clasped the other to his chest. The audience applauded enthusiastically at this first sign of actual acting. Then Cecil toppled off the stage into the lap of his surprised friend Brogan. In that one shocked moment, Brogan let Cecil's inert body drop to the floor, an entirely understandable reaction to seeing his own dreams of stardom evaporate along with Cecil's final breath.

With his leather-goods business gone, Brogan tried to obtain a loan at the big black marble bank. Brogan attempted to leverage his legitimacy by boasting of his close friendship with the erstwhile high-level executive of the bank, Cecil. The bank rep checked on his computer and said there was not now, and nor had there ever been, any record of any employee, executive or otherwise, by that name.

BUNNY THE THREADBARE PARROT

Marli had linked an entire jumbo box of paperclips together. "Look what Marli did!" said Chester smugly to his father, eager for Marli to get into trouble. Edgar just said "Tsk! Tsk!" and dumped the sixteen-foot-long chain on the receptionist's desk.

"Get that untangled," he said, and grabbed each twin's hand. His assistant Mary Sue trotted out the door behind them.

Mary Sue buckled the children into the back seat and placed toys around them.

Edgar was grinning, rubbing his hands together.

"This is the big one," he said. "I'm about to pick up the signed paperwork!"

Mary Sue smiled, "Oh, congratulations, Gar, this is a huge sale for you, the biggest ever."

"It will be in a few minutes," Edgar said, trying not to gloat. He turned his attention to the traffic.

Marli was squirming, looking around her. "Where's Bunny?" she said.

Edgar glanced back over his shoulder. "Bunny the lobster is right there next to you."

"No! I don't want Bunny Lob Lob, I want the OTHER Bunny!" Marli's voice rose.

"Look, there's Bunny the red dog." Mary Sue hoped to avert a tantrum.

"No!" Marli spotted a pink foot peeking out from under Chester's leg.

"CHESTER IS SITTING ON BUNNY!" she screamed.

Edgar pulled over. Mary Sue ran to the back and retrieved the hapless Bunny from under a grinning Chester. They set off again.

Marli looked out the window. "The new nanny quit," she announced to no one in particular.

Edgar's elbow was leaning on the console between the front seats, but the rest of his arm disappeared into Mary Sue's lap.

Marli added, "Mommy was ever so angry." Edgar was preoccupied with traffic. Mary Sue was preoccupied with Edgar's wandering fingers.

Marli continued her story. "Mommy said to Daddy well *you* deal, because *I'm* going shopping."

"Oh, Gar, did she really? Oh, I am so sorry!" Mary Sue squeezed Edgar's hand. "Daphne always manages to upset the nannies, doesn't she."

"Yep. Daphne caused the usual chaos," Edgar said, playing the victim.

"Cows? Cows?" Marli's voice was shrill. "The cows will eat Bunny the parrot!"

Mary Sue said, "There are no cows, Marli." To Edgar she said, "That's eight or nine nannies now, isn't it?"

"They come and go so fast, who the hell knows." Edgar was feeling mellow. He was anticipating his big payday.

"But to go shopping. I mean Daphne should at least have watched the twins today, seeing as you had this big sale, hmm?" Mary Sue was mining the issue to the max.

"Daddy said all Mommy does is shop shop shop," said Marli, trying to be part of the conversation.

Edgar and Mary Sue exchanged little private smiles.

Visions of living in a vast stately mansion pirouetted in Edgar's head. He was thinking today's commission would be his ticket to a tree-lined, high-income street, and classy neighbors. His phone rang. He adjusted his ear buds. He listened for a moment, then sputtered incredulously, "What do you mean the seller walked! Didn't they see our Counter?"

Chester started to kick the back of Mary Sue's seat, rhythmically drumming one foot after the other. Mary Sue didn't say anything.

Edgar's voice rose an octave. "Just tell your clients to counter our Counter!"

Bored and ignored, Chester reached over and pinched Marli's leg. Marli capitalized on this latest outrage immediately. She shrieked, "Daddy, Daddy, look what Chester is doing to me!"

Mary Sue cooed at Marli, "What's wrong, what's the matter Sweetie?" She hoped Edgar would notice how good she was with his children.

Marli ignored her and screamed more loudly,

"DADDY, DADDY, LOOK WHAT CHESTER IS DOING TO ME!"

Edgar shouted, "Chester, for God's sake stop it!" He adjusted his tone and said ingratiatingly into his cell, "Look, I'm nearly there, we can talk, can't we?"

Marli discovered how to flip the window up and down. The breeze rearranged Mary Sue's careful hairdo, but she didn't say anything. Since nobody remarked on Marli's new skill, she threw Bunny the lobster out the window.

In case anyone missed it, Chester announced loudly, "Marli threw Lob Lob out the window."

Mary Sue turned around and cooed to Chester, "What Sweetie?"

Chester said rudely, "I'm not talking to you. Daddy, MARLI THREW LOB LOB OUT THE WINDOW!"

Edgar was trying to reason with the seller's agent.

"What do you mean they got a much higher offer. How much higher? Yes, it *is* my business!"

Chester resumed kicking Mary Sue's seat, "Marli (bam) threw (bam) Lob Lob (bam) ..."

Mary Sue still didn't say anything, she didn't want to appear to be a grouch. Edgar said to her irritably, "That rat hung up on me! What's the matter with Chester now?"

Mary Sue tried to explain. "Chester said Marli threw the lob ..."

"Threw the laptop ...? Oh no, it's got all my private shit on it ..." Edgar swerved abruptly and hit the curb with a jolt. He motioned to Mary Sue. "Go look for it!" He punched numbers on his cellphone. "Please just wait, just let my people make another offer to your clients."

Mary Sue got out and teetered back along the road on her fashionably high heels.

"Marli did it," Chester whined hopefully.

His father was talking fast on his cell, "I'm sure all my client needs is a little extra time, just ..."

In a last-ditch effort to get some satisfaction, Chester shouted, "MARLI THREW THE LAPTOP OUT!"

Edgar angrily whirled around to face his son.

"Chester, stop that godawful shouting! Stop it!" He turned up the sound on his cell. "Please, just a bit more time."

Chester fell back, chin wobbling, eyes filling. His thumb found his mouth, and he hunched into the far corner of the seat. Mary Sue came back and climbed in the car. She said triumphantly, "Look Marli, I found Bunny Lob Lob!"

Marli pretended to be asleep. And Mary Sue noticed that the laptop was tucked safely into a seat pocket next to an empty bottle of Grecian Formula.

Edgar squealed tires back out into traffic, eyes darting nervously to the car clock.

"I hope the traffic isn't too bad," said Mary Sue.

"Yes, sir, yes," Edgar said, fawning deferentially into his cell phone. His yellow real estate jacket now had wet armpits. "I am VERY sure I can persuade my client to beat their price." His eyes swiveled to the clock. "Yes, I know you can just mail the rejection to me, but I would rather … the deadline passed? But I will be there in five minutes!" His voice was pleading, groveling. Anyone else might have been ashamed to be begging like that, but by then Edgar was talking to himself anyway, the phone had gone dead.

"We'll never make it in five minutes," Mary Sue said.

Edgar started weaving violently in and out of the traffic. Mary Sue clutched the dash with both hands. Marli was firmly wedged between Bunny the red dog, Bunny Lob Lob, and Bunny the pink rabbit, but Chester was being tossed from side to side and growing queasier by the minute. Something sour had already risen to his throat when Edgar took a corner at 60. Chester hurled.

Edgar screeched to a stop, and immediately got on his phone. He implored pitifully, "I'm still on my way but I just got a little bit delayed, I had to bring the children to work today …"

It was a company car so nobody was concerned with the interior, but Mary Sue was doing what she could for Chester with bottled water on the sidewalk. Edgar stumbled over to them, his shoulders drooping, heavy with the pain of seeing his big commission and stately mansion disappear.

"They accepted a higher offer," he muttered.

"Oh Gar, I am so sorry." Mary Sue stroked his cheek. "It's all Daphne's fault," she added, in case Edgar had lost sight of the real villain.

Chester thought his condition should elicit some much-needed sympathy. He pushed his advantage. "I want an ice cream," he announced.

"Get in the fucking car," his father said.

Edgar gripped the wheel, face grim. "Let's not go back to the office."

Mary Sue nodded happily.

A few minutes later Edgar swung the car into his driveway and quickly pulled into the garage to avoid prying eyes.

Too late. Harriet was already at her window. Harriett was always at her window. Nothing escaped her notice in that cramped cul-de-sac of small shoulder to shoulder houses. She could see into Edgar's car just as clearly as she could see into Edgar's living room.

She could see Bunny the parrot rouse himself at the sound of the car.

Bunny spent his nights in a cage, but during the day he was shackled to a small roost near the window. He dozed off a lot, probably due to his advanced age. He would topple over and hang upside down by one ankle, fast asleep. The cat would seize the opportunity to creep up and use his sharp teeth to pluck out Bunny's feathers. This woke Bunny with a start, and affronted and insulted, Bunny would flap back up onto his perch screeching indignantly, "Shop shop shop, all she does is shop." Harriet would watch this drama daily.

Edgar called Rush More Pizza and placed an order and Mary Sue settled the children on the couch next to the cat and turned on the TV.

"Shop shop shop, all she does is shop," squawked Bunny, as SpongeBob Square Pants lit up the screen.

Edgar and Mary Sue tiptoed upstairs.

The doorbell rang.

There were giggles from upstairs.

Clearly nobody was coming down.

"Shop shop shop, all she does is shop," screeched Bunny.

Chester slid off the couch, and with a sly glance at Marli, he unclipped Bunny's leg shackle, and went to the front door. He opened it very wide and waited.

The delivery boy leaned in with a professional smile, one hand ready to receive a tip. Bunny felt a breeze and slowly turned his head. He gazed sleepily at the open door. He was clearly thinking things over.

Chester waited.

The Rush More Pizza delivery boy waited.

Then in a burst of unusually robust flapping, Bunny filled the entryway and was gone. The delivery boy ducked. Chester grabbed the pizza and slammed the door.

He went back to the couch and graciously offered Marli the first slice.

Three minutes later, Daphne's cell phone rang.

"Daphne dear …"

"Oh Harriet! You should come to Nordy's, there's 50% off …"

"Daphne dear, Bunny got out."

"… bras in the lingerie dep … what?" Pause. "You said Bunny got out?"

"Yes, dear. Bunny got out." Harriet was loving this.

"Bunny got *out*? Oh my God, no! Marli will be hysterical. We tried to get rid of him once because he's so ugly, he's hardly got any feathers left, but Marli screamed for a week, he's her parrot you know …"

Harriet interrupted Daphne's rambling. "He's sitting on my front gate. I think he's asleep."

"Oh, no, a dog will get him …"

"Yes, very likely. Or a coyote. Or a raccoon." Harriet relished the moment. "You'd really better come home right away, Daphne."

"Oh my god, Harriet. I'm coming, I'm coming …"

Daphne pulled up her car in front of Harriet's house. Bunny, who by some miracle had retained his grip on the gate, was nodding and leaning dangerously. Daphne grabbed him and tucked him under her arm and marched across the cul-de-sac to her house.

Harriet got a fresh cup of coffee and settled at her front window to watch.

MUM

Mum, Mum, I'm home!"

No answer. I walk down the familiar hallway, still calling, "Mum, I'm home." No answer. The kitchen is at the back of the house. I walk all the way back there and stop in the doorway. She's sitting at the kitchen table with her back to me. She has a cup of tea in front of her. I walk in. It feels the same, it smells the same.

"Mum, I'm home!"

She doesn't look up. "You were shtoopit ven you were ten, and you are shtoopit now. And all of your degrees don't make any difference. You are no better than you was."

The gut punch is familiar. Against my better judgement, I sit down opposite her. I want to change the script; I want to rewrite it and turn it into a story about a happy homecoming. I find myself babbling a mile a minute to erase that look from her face, waiting for a spark of interest. I want to connect with her, have her ask about my journey. I go on and on filling the air about travelling for 24 hours, how they held the plane at Los Angeles because storms had delayed my flight from Connecticut. How they told everyone to stay seated, and they called my name for just me to come up to the front, and how a flight attendant ran with me to the international gate, and how the Qantas flight had waited and how all the passengers had clapped when I made it on board, and how we were all herded into a hangar at Townsville so they could scrub and disinfect the plane before we could take off for Melbourne.

I am out of breath.

The air hangs heavy.

Finally, she says, "American schools are no good."

Gunter shows up the next morning at 9 o'clock. Mum tries to give him some importance by introducing him as "Herr…" but he waves that aside and says, "Just call me Gunter." His accent is as thick as hers. As a young sailor he had jumped ship in the port of Sydney to escape Hitler's Germany. After the introductions and pleasantries, Gunter settles in, taking my father's chair at the kitchen table.

Without much preamble, my mother gets to the point of why she invited me to visit her.

"I vant you to move here and take care off me," she says. Her w's are still v's, her of is still pronounced off.

"Well, I am just rattling around in a big old house in Connecticut. You could come and live with me," I say.

"We have sign painters here," Günter says quickly, taking charge, before my mother can speak.

"I don't paint signs." Günter looks baffled. I say, "I am Director of Marketing …"

Günter resumes control. "Oh, we have supermarkets here," he says.

"You could be a cashier at zee supermarket," my mother says. They nod together, a united front. She looks at me smugly. "You must really be sorry you moved to America," she says.

"No, it's the best thing I ever did," I say.

She twists her mouth, letting me know she doesn't believe me. "I gave her the money to go to America," she tells Gunter.

I say, "No you didn't, I was up in Queensland, remember? You didn't even know I was going. I worked three jobs to save up the money."

Gunter looks uncomfortable.

My mother wants to make sure he is still on her side. "Günter's wife won't let him in the house during the day. She complains he vipes his dirty hands on zee towels. So, he comes here."

Gunter glances at her gratefully; it's established, he is the victim of injustice. They have the enemy pegged.

"We don't have sex or anything," he says to me.

"I don't need to know, Günter."

There is an awkward silence.

Then my mother blurts out suddenly, "Your father and me vas very much in luff!" That's something she wants to get established right away, that's her story. Her timing is off, but she makes her point. I remember all the times my father shouted at her to go back to wherever she came from, so I am silent, staring hard at her. She avoids my gaze, her eyes are moist, she is playing it to the hilt.

Günter gallops in on cue. "Your Dad loved your Mum very much," he says. "She was a wonderful wife and mother."

My mother's eyes are spiteful. "You vill never be a wife and mother. Nobody vill ever marry you now."

"Yes Mum, so you mentioned every day when I was growing up. But I did get married."

"He would haff married anybody."

"You never met him."

"You never gave your mother any grandchildren," Gunter says accusingly, trying to make points with her.

"She doesn't like children. She locked me out of the house even when it was freezing and pouring rain."

I don't want to say very much about it, I have never let strangers into our personal business. I know Gunter wants us to fight so that she won't choose me. He's afraid she'll come to live with me in America.

Gunter hangs out here every day, they speak German together. Even with me here for such a short visit, he shows up every morning at 9 o'clock, on the pretext of bringing us a bottle of milk. He sits here with us all day. He isn't going to give my mother and me a moment to talk privately.

"You look just like your father," Günter says, making conversation. Bad choice.

"Yes, I know. I take after him," I say, watching my mother's face turn purple and become thunderous at such blasphemy. I rub it in. "We are a lot alike. He was a reader, he had thousands of books, and I love to read too."

"Your father said you are shtoopit!" She spits it out.

When he died, she didn't let me know about it for months. It was as though she needed to keep me from the funeral, she wouldn't have wanted my father to know I was there for him. While she is trying to think of something to smooth over her outburst for Günter's benefit, I keep going.

"He always used to get the Saturday Evening Post. That's why I became interested in going to America, and so did he." My mother glares at me. I ignore her and say to Günter, "He came over to visit me and my husband in Connecticut."

Gunter is looking at my mother, not sure what would be advantageous for him to say right now.

She snaps at me, "Well, your husband divorced you!"

"And Dad was going to divorce you. Only he had a heart attack before he could do it."

There, it was said. Gunter glances at my mother, his mouth is looking for words. My mother's face is stricken.

I shrug, and tell her, "You knew. He said he told you he was going to divorce you and go to America. He said you found his passport and travel documents and tried to destroy them."

The next morning, I get up early. I feel stiff and cramped from sitting in the small kitchen every day. I know my mother isn't going to go on any walks with me. She is way over-weight; she is as wide as she is tall. I steal out of the house and pause on the front step and breathe in deeply. The air is so sweet, warm already at this early hour, crackling with insect buzz and wakening bird calls. I stretch a bit, and then take off. I am pounding the pavement, running, running, running, just running. Finally, I feel ready to go back. I arrive at the gate just as Gunter is coming with the unnecessary bottle of milk.

"She only uses it in her tea, you don't need to bring one every day," I tell him.

He looks as though he is going to cry, his bottom lip is trembling. I pat his shoulder reassuringly and we go in. My mother is sitting at the kitchen table, her hat and coat on, even though it is 80 out.

"I vanted to go to zee shops," she says sulkily.

I ignore her tone. "No problem," I say. "I'm all sweaty, just let me take a quick bath, and we can go."

I can hear them talking in German while I am in the bathroom. I emerge all clean and refreshed and walk into the kitchen. They are sitting close together side by side.

I say cheerily, "OK, we can go now if you are ready."

My mother looks up and glowers at me. Gunter is examining the table closely.

"You want to go now?" I say, keeping my voice bubbly. I sense this is a war zone. There are snipers here with me in their sights. "What's wrong?" I say stupidly.

My mother stands up abruptly. Her chair tips over and crashes to the floor. She draws herself up till the top of her head is level with my chest. Her eyes are glinting, and she takes a big breath; her malevolent stare does not waver.

"Günter said you tried to cuddle him!"

Gunter is just sitting there. The table has never been more fascinating to him.

"I patted him on the shoulder," I say to my mother. The air is thick, charged. Gunter is holding his breath.

I slump down into a chair. "Mum, you have got to get over this competition thing. Geez, you even tried to keep me away from my father when I was four! You said little girls like me always try to steal their daddies away from their mummies, remember?"

My mother says nothing. She is scowling at me with decades-old fury.

Next morning before the first bird chirps, I pack my few belongings and tiptoe down the hall, just as I had as a 15-year-old, many years ago. I hear her bed creak as I open the front door, but she doesn't try to stop me.

Two years later, I am back for her funeral. She is buried next to my father; she now has him for eternity. She must be gloating about that, though how he would feel about it is another matter. There is a single red rose lying on her grave. I wonder if Gunter brings her one each morning, just like he did with the bottle of milk.

RESISTANCE

I was choking, coughing, gagging in the acrid air. My breath came in shallow gasps and there was a sour taste in my mouth. Fighting panic, I tried to rise to my knees, only to crack my head on a beam. My eyes burned as I strained to see. I heard a strange high-pitched sound, and realized it was my own voice, whimpering. Ash and dirt fell like continuous silent rain. I could hear my heart pounding. I felt around me, timidly at first, then more feverishly, the splintered walls slashing my hands as I tried to gauge the limits of my prison. Then suddenly something was creaking. It started as a slight squeak, then grew louder. Water began to drip steadily, soaking me. Terror knotted my stomach as my fingers frantically tore at wood and concrete. I found a gap and clawed at it, widening it enough to allow me to ease in sideways, and then wriggle wormlike along the narrow passage. Disoriented, groping blindly, I grasped at anything to get traction. The creaking was growing ever louder above me, compelling me to keep going, but then I felt my strength flag, I felt myself slowing, I was running out of steam.

A sudden weak gust of air gave me promise of an opening, and with a renewed burst of energy I fought my way toward it. Finally, soaked and shattered, I gave one last tremendous push, and then strong hands grabbed me and pulled me free.

"Elle est morte ? Non, elle vie! Vite!"

I collapsed in their arms, totally spent. A blanket was tucked around me and a moist cloth wiped my nose and eyes. Several hands lifted me, and then I was aware of no more.

I was jolted awake by a harsh, guttural voice.

"So where is your boyfriend?"

A strong odor of antiseptic filled my nostrils. I felt as though I was lying on a bed of bricks, the rough sheets irritated my bruised skin. Bandages covered my head. I could see a white-uniformed nurse moving about at the other end of the room.

I was at eye-level with his gold jacket buttons.

He had to repeat his question. "I said where is your boyfriend?"

"Boyfriend? I don't have a boyfriend."

"Yes, you do." He held a photograph close to my face. "Where is he now?"

My eyes hurt from the blazing overhead lights. I focused with difficulty on the picture. It had been taken in the club.

"I don't know. He just came over and talked to me. I had never seen him before."

"You were holding hands. You hold hands with every stranger, you're a *Schlampe*, you're a *Strassenfrau*? So, what did he say to you, this boyfriend?"

"He tried to tell me I had to leave. Then he went to the bathroom."

"There were no bodies in the bathroom."

"Well, he stood up and said very loudly that he was going to the bathroom. Anyone could hear."

"Yes, he is very clever. And then he slipped out of the club. We already know he is a Resistance fighter; we were watching him. Don't play with me. He left you to die. You are protecting a murderer."

He suddenly grabbed my arm and wrenched it upward. I screamed with pain. Cold metal clattered against the bedframe as it snapped on my wrist.

"You will not be going anywhere. I will be back. Maybe you will have had some time to think, *Schlampe*."

The staccato clacking of his boots on the concrete floor grew fainter.

He had left the photo lying on my bedsheet. You could see in the photo I was looking sideways at the man holding my hand, a clearly very doubtful expression on my face. Now I realized his overcoat showed he was dressed for the street, not to spend an evening in a club.

The place had been full of Germans. The air was thick with cigarette smoke, and smelled of bratwurst, fried potatoes, and cabbage. The noise was deafening. There was a singer, but she was drowned out by raucous drunken voices.

Trink, trink, Brüderlein trink,
Lass doch die Sorgen zu Haus!

I suppose my housemate had chosen to meet here because it was the closest club to our flat. It wasn't a good idea to be out late far from home, the streets were patrolled. We had been desperate to pretend for just a few hours it was like old times in gay Paris. But as soon as I got to the club, I saw the Germans, and I wanted to turn around and leave, but then she would have come and waited for me. So, I took a stool at the bar, as far from the Germans as I could. Flashbulbs went off continually, the Germans were photographing their good times.

Trink, trink, Brüderlein trink,
Zieh doch die Stirn nicht so kraus

He slid onto the stool beside me.

I said quickly, "That seat is taken, someone is coming, I'm waiting for somebody."

He reached for my hand as though we were friends and leaned forward. "Don't make a fuss," he said, inclining his head toward the Germans. "You need to leave here now."

"Who are you?" I blurted.

Meide den Kummer und meide den Schmerz,
Dann ist das Leben ein Scherz!

"Just go. Leave now." He stood up and said in an unnaturally loud voice that he was going to the bathroom. And then he was gone.

I remember looking about me, unsure what to do.

O du lieber Augustine, Augustine, Augustine
O du lieber Augustine, Alles is weg.

And that is when the explosion turned everything black.

AS IF

EDGAR BARRY, REAL ESTATE

That's what the sign on the door said, though there had not been much of that going on lately. It was the preppy Ivy-League real estate agents, or those lucky enough to look and sound like them, who got 90% of the business. Edgar was not among that golden few. He was relegated to scratching for the scraps. As a result, he took every client who walked in the door, people that other agents refused to work with. Edgar took the over-extended, the under-funded, the clients with complicated divorces, and the clients whose dreams did not match their wallets or their prospects. A shortage of ethics characterized them all, shady characters flying just under the legal radar.

And thus, they were a good match for Edgar. Most of his transactions were cobbled together by questionable and tenuous means. His own ethics were creatively tweaked and molded to suit the occasion or the client. The facts of Edgar's biography morphed to fit the requirement of the situation. He reinvented himself daily to impress. Even so, the sour-faced landlord visited him each week and would only take the rent in cash, and Edgar was now down to his last two employees, a bookkeeper, and Mary Sue who was his assistant and somewhat more, but nobody asked.

His twins were in a private pre-school he couldn't afford, funded by financial aid which he told people was a scholarship, and he had recently managed to stitch together with promises and IOUs the ability to move into a house far above his income level on a good day.

He had named his children Marylebone and Chesterfield, thinking the posh names would impress. But the other children in their expensive school simply called them Mari and Che. They couldn't pronounce Marylebone and Chesterfield, but Mari and Che were names they knew, those were the names of their Hispanic nannies, house cleaners and gardeners.

Edgar longed to enter the rarified air of society in his new suburb. But so far only the grandfather of one of his neighbors had spoken to him. The old man was out on his walker one day with a nursing aide and had mistaken Edgar for the gardener. The old man had given him detailed instructions on how to prune roses.

Edgar's many attempts to raise money to finance his new lifestyle had so far fallen flat. Family was out of the question, in fact they often called him looking for a handout. He had approached a former client, a man with a waterfront home, a boat, and a fleet of late model cars. Edgar presented to him a vague investment idea to fund a project that had not quite come together yet. The client was not impressed. Edgar was then forced to beg, plead, flatter, and grovel. The client remained unmoved, mumbling something about all his cash being tied up in property.

Truth be told, the client's situation was much the same as Edgar's.

His bookkeeper was, of course, horrified as a desperate Edgar started to approach loan sharks, though so far even they had not been interested. All Edgar's phone calls and faxes to the loan sharks brought him to the attention of someone else. A letter popped out of the fax machine.

Attention Mister Barry:

Good morning. First of all let me introduce myself. My name is Mrs. Sabado. I work with Banco Sabado Atlantico. I have a confidential business proposal I am contacting you about, in regards to our deceased client, who was a victim of a car accident who happens to bear the same SURNAME with you. Before his death, our client deposited the sum of ($21,000,00,00 USD) Twenty One of Millions United State of American Dollars, with our Bank. Documentations regarding this indicate that he had no will or outstanding instructions in regards to this deposit before his death. For this reason, I can present you as the next of kin based on the fact that you bear the same SURNAME with our late client. Nobody is coming for this deposit and we are sure that he died with his entire family and relatives. I have put in place all the necessary documentations concerning the release of this deposit fund to you. Upon your acceptance to cooperate with me, I agree that 40% of this deposit money will be for you as a foreign partner, while 50% will be for me and my colleague here in our office, while 10% will be mapped out for charity donations. For security & confidential reasons, I strongly advise that you contact me immediately you receive this letter with your Private Telephone number, your Bank Account number, and your own Social Security Number. I GUARANTEE that this process will be executed under a legitimate arrangement that will legally protect you from any breach of law. Thank you and I urgently look forward to hear from you.

Yours, Sincerely.

Mrs. Sabado. Banker & Manager

Edgar had come to the fax machine to send off yet another panicked loan shark application, when he saw the letter. He picked it up, read it, frowned, and read it again. His face lit up as he absorbed the information. He whirled around and held it out to Mary Sue. He said excitedly, "Look, look at this! Some relative of mine died, and the bank says I'm next of kin. They've got $21 million of his money, and it says I am to get 40%! Let's see …" he did a quick calculation "… I'd get over $8 million!"

Mary Sue read the letter and was genuinely thrilled for him. "Oh, Gar, that's wonderful! You are saved!"

The bookkeeper was nearby, head and shoulders into a cabinet, filing unpaid bills. Edgar flapped the letter in her direction, smug and triumphant. He felt she had always been unnecessarily critical of his finances. She took the letter and read it through. When she finished, she looked up at his shining happy face. His mouth hung open with expectation.

"But Edgar," she said, "Your name is Edgardo Barriento. Your last name isn't Barry and never was, you made that up to get more business."

That took him a moment to absorb. Then his face crumpled. The bookkeeper had to go back to her filing, she couldn't bear to look at him.

Edgar's lips quivered but he said quickly, his voice cracking, "I knew that."

Mary Sue was quick to touch his arm sympathetically. "Oh, Gar Babe," she said. "I'm so sorry. You know those new earrings I wanted? well you don't need to buy them for me this week."

THE PROMISED LAND

U tter, complete, mind-crushing boredom was my only excuse. I was crouched in a corner of the Twenty-Nine Palms library deep into a beautifully illustrated book about Joshua Tree National Park.

"Interested in a trip out there?"

His voice was cheerful, friendly, casual. He said his name was Wally, he didn't give a last name, but his khakis immediately made me connect him with the Marine Corp Air Ground Combat base. A common complaint among the 20,000 servicemen stationed there at that isolated outpost was that there was nothing to do, so for that reason alone, he and I had something in common. I had just got word that my Director and camera crew were delayed yet another day in Los Angeles. I said yes to him without hesitation.

I stepped out of the air-conditioned hotel into the blast-furnace late afternoon heat and gasped at the gleaming silver mile-high open top Jeep Gladiator at the curb.

"So, you brought a tank from the Base?"

Wally threw back his head and laughed. He looked as though he was performing in a TV Colgate toothpaste commercial.His teeth were too straight, too white.

"Nice teeth," I said.

"My God-given natural-born Hollywood teeth," he bragged.

"Yeah, right!" I snorted. Being a smart mouth had never scared away the men who wanted to be seen with a model.

He took a knee so that I could climb up into the Jeep. I could feel his taut muscles through the Army camo. It was not the current Woodland design, or even the brown-beige desert issue of local Marines, but instead it was the vintage Vietnam-era ERDL green and tan. A cigarette pack was rolled into his sleeve. He made a big show of working the gear stick for the benefit of the people gaping at us and we pulled into the early evening traffic.

We only went as far as the nearest gas station.

I needled him. "You gassed up on base and this guzzler ate up a tank between there and my hotel?"

"Nah, I had to go to Palm Springs this morning." He didn't elaborate.

At the pump, he filled up next to a portly silver-haired senior in a red T-shirt, the white letters CHUBBY BUT SEXY stretched across his stomach. The oldster tipped back his Stetson and call out to Wally, "Nice ride."

"Yeah, I just bought it."

"You install a lift? What are those, 37s?"

"Came with. Extreme terrain. Supercharged V8, steel bumpers, LED package. Loaded, and the bed's got room for two dirt bikes." Wally swaggered as he replaced the pump.

"Gotta be sixty thou, right? Rough in the city?" The senior was persistent.

"Nah, she's got outstanding street manners."

When the hoped-for offer didn't come, the man looked wistful. "Well, I'd sure like to go for a spin in that."

"Sure thing," said Wally. "Catch you later!"

We cleared town, radio blaring, and instead of going to the nearest Park entrance, Wally turned left onto 62. Ahead lay an open stretch of two-lane highway, and he gunned it. It felt like a rocket taking off. White memorial crosses lining the road flashed by in a blur. I clenched my teeth and hung on. I think I dug ten finger-holes into my bucket seat. Wally made a sudden squealing right onto 177, right again at 10, and sped along the southern border of the Park. He whipped past the Cottonwood entrance and a few minutes later he jerked the wheel hard right onto Dillon, then onto Berdoo. The paved road had ended, and we were bouncing on a rocky pitted trail. A yellow sign warned "4WD only" and "at your own risk." An SUV behind us turned around when they saw the brutal terrain. Not so Wally. Where jagged rocks and fresh slides blocked the way, even with the steep canyon walls on each side limiting his options, Wally recklessly created alternate routes. He only laughed when I screamed, he was enjoying himself and my discomfort.

Eventually the stark rock walls fell away, opening to endless, bleak, flat and featureless wasteland. The trail stretched ahead for miles. Wally careened deeper into the wilderness, spewing up clouds of sand and gravel. When the track forked, he pulled the wheel so sharply that he skidded several feet and almost took out the only road sign. More Joshuas and different shades of gray-green vegetation didn't relieve the harsh endless terrain.

Without warning, Wally suddenly left the track and began to hurtle across uncharted territory. He was like a man possessed, fiercely yanking the wheel to dodge bushes, rocks and Joshuas. He suddenly slid to a halt, cut the engine, and sat back. He looked hugely proud of himself, smug at his power and control over the machine.

"Where are we?" I asked.

"Joshua. I promised you Joshua, and now you've got Joshua. "He lit a cigarette and inhaled deeply. "Ah, that's good, I haven't eaten all day." He took a last drag and flicked the butt. "You down for a hike?"

"No, I am not," I said. "My eyes and nose are filled with dust, and I ache all over. Take me back to the hotel."

"Nope." He looked me up and down. "So, you look real fake with all that makeup. D'you make a lot of money?"

"Enough that I don't have to come in the back way to the Park to avoid the entrance fee."

He snickered and vaulted out of the jeep. "Just a little walk, don't be a wuss," he said.

I looked around and saw only the flat monotony of colorless desert, broken by monstrous heaps of haphazardly piled boulders. It didn't look like the colorful library book.

"I don't see a hiking trail," I said.

"Don't need a trail. I'm Special Forces. We've all got these." He pointed to the large piece of modern technology strapped to his wrist.

I blurted out, "You're Special Forces? I thought they were all down at LeJeune."

He ignored me and walked away from the rocks to a clear space to calibrate his GPS. His T-shirt was wet across the back and armpits.

I clicked open the glove compartment hoping to find a Park map. What I found was an elegant moss-green folder with a flashy gold logo. It looked familiar. It was a brochure from an upscale and expensive Palm Springs vehicle rental company. My agency had often rented a Lamborghini by the hour for Palm Springs shoots. I lifted the flap. The name on the contract was not "Wally." I reached under my seat for my backpack, dragging out with it a colorful empty cardboard box. Emblazoned in block letters on all four sides were the words:

BEST HIKING WATCH! ALTIMETER, BAROMETER, COMPASS, GPS!

I kicked the box back under the seat, and with deep misgivings, climbed down. The late afternoon heat sizzled off the rocks, and my cotton dress clung to me. I considered finding my way out of the Park alone, but the utter desolation of our surroundings bound me to him. And he knew it. He ignored me.

I walked over to him. Something was not going well with his big watch, I could tell. I tried to humor him. "I bet that does everything but polish your boots and tie the laces."

He was frowning and prodding and fiddling with it, concentrating. I wanted to say the instructions are in the car but thought better of it. When he was done, his gaze fell on my backpack. His lip curled. OK, so it was pink plastic with frilly pink arm straps, and I bought it because it matched my dress. Wally looked disgusted. "More makeup? You don't need whatever's in that! I'm an expert survivalist." He whirled and set off at a brisk pace. I called out to him to watch for the abandoned mine shafts I'd read about in the book, but he didn't hear. I adjusted my sunhat, and with my thin cotton dress flapping against my legs, ran after him. I had always thought I was reasonably fit, but two years as a cheerleader had not prepared me for this. I could not keep up with him. He leaped over bushes, darted around tall cactus plants, ducked under outcrops. It was as though he was on his own imaginary military expedition.

At one point he stopped abruptly and knelt down, pointing, waiting for me, his voice excited.

"Look, there's bones! Do you know what they are?"

"A woolly mammoth?" I caught up, totally out of breath.

He shot me a withering look. "No, it's a human body. A lot of people have been murdered out here. That dumb hat is lame." He reached up and knocked it off my head.

He kicked at the bones and took off again. He didn't bother to slow his pace or even look to see if I was behind him. He didn't notice when I paused often to take sips of water and munch on Nature Bars. I caught up when he stopped to recalibrate his GPS. He was sitting on a splintered mineshaft wall, tugging at the strap where it was chaffing his wet wrist. He lit a cigarette. Sweat was dripping in his eyes.

He looked around. "Us Marines know how to get water out of the desert."

He jumped up and darted across the sand to the edge of an arroyo, took a penknife from his pocket, and began to stab at a barrel cactus. Its ridges were covered with three-inch lethal-looking spines. He gasped as thorns pierced his hand. He sucked at the wounds but continued stabbing at the cactus. He finally sat back on his heels. He looked quite crestfallen. I think he expected cactus water to gush out, like in the movies. He stood up and with one angry swipe he hacked off the top of the cactus. What he found inside was a pulpy white mass. He swore, and then sawed at the flesh, stuffing it in his mouth. He sucked and chewed at it ravenously, and then he brushed the back of his hand across his mouth as though he had eaten a satisfying meal. I could tell that he was gagging.

"Want some?" he held out a fistful to me.

"Um, no thanks." He eyes narrowed so I quickly added, "It looks good, I'll have some later."

He took off again, running at the same frenetic pace. I dawdled far enough behind him to eat my last Nature Bar and drink the rest of my water. He was talking to himself as I caught up. He tapped at the watch, listened to it, then started punching it aggressively.

"Problem?" I asked.

"Shut up," he snapped, "I've got it under control."

He sucked at his puncture wounds and tugged at the uncomfortable watch band. He started out again, detouring toward a shallow wash to attack another barrel cactus. He hacked at it, viciously tearing off chunks. He got to his feet with difficulty, chewing, but was unable to stop grimacing.

"See?" he said, swallowing with difficulty. "Us Special Forces can survive in the desert." He looked around. "There's water in the Joshuas, they're succulents, they hold water, and they've got fruit at the top."

I couldn't see any fruit on those spikey fists, but I followed him. He tried to climb up, clinging to the fibrous bark. He fell twice, then fell again, and rolled on his back, breathing heavily. His hair was plastered to his forehead, his face was the color of putty.

To cover the awkward moment, I tried a bit of light conversation. "The Mormons thought these trees looked like the biblical Joshua pointing the way to the Promised Land. More like luring travelers into the mouth of Hell."

"That's so dumb." He closed his eyes to shut me out.

I held up my hand to the horizon. I had learned from the Joshua Tree book that if I counted how many pinkie finger widths from the bottom of the sun to the horizon, I could tell when the sun would set.

I told him, "The sun will be gone in about a half hour. It will be totally dark soon."

"You don't know what you're talking about." He struggled to his feet. He didn't notice the Jeep key fob fall out of his pocket. I quickly scooped it up and tucked it in my bra. I reached out to help him, but he pushed me aside. He was eyeing my pink backpack. "Did you bring any water?"

"Um, water?" I was all innocence.

His lip tightened. "You dumb fuck, where did you think we were going, Disneyland? Dumb fake model."

"Dumb fake Marine."

That lit him like a match. He shrieked, "Give me your bag!" He wrenched it off my back, and eagerly upended my water bottle. Barely a drop fell into his mouth.

He lunged for me, his knife an inch from my eye.

"You drunk it all! I'm gonna cut you so bad you'll never see another camera!" But suddenly he was seized by a fit of vomiting, bending over and retching. I kneed him hard in the groin. He yelped, and I took off running.

I didn't even feel the thorn bushes tearing at my bare legs as I ran. I could hardly distinguish between a shadow and a hole in that faint light. Wally's weakened condition gave me a head start, but I could hear his ragged breath right behind me, and then he was so close I could feel his body heat. In the gloom I spotted the wooden boards, barely visible, almost hidden under bushes. In the split second that I jumped aside, Wally lunged. His foot hit the rotted wood. There was a loud crack as it gave way, and he disappeared into the ground. The desert had swallowed him.

I sat down heavily, fighting to catch my breath. The sun slipped further below the horizon, and the orange blaze that had fanned across the sky slowly faded. Night had closed its fist. I couldn't see much; I needed a better vantage point. I circled a massive boulder until in the hazy light I could pick out a way up. I groped my way to the top, feeling very fragile and close to tears clinging to that desert rock.

The boulders that had been ablaze in the sunset's fiery glow were now ghostly white dots, they looked like globs of candle wax on the surreal landscape. I caught sight of something glinting in that weak moonlight. It had to be the Jeep. If it was, we had come surprisingly close. My arms and legs ached with the effort of holding on, but I had to dig deep to pry my hands loose and start on the descent. My heart was pounding hard enough to jump out of my chest and my entire body was shaking when my feet hit flat ground.

The Jeep started, and I eased it forward. The night was clear, the stars were visible. I knew Twenty-Nine Palms lay along the north side of the Park, and that was the direction I needed to go. I could make out the Big Dipper and its two pointer stars, and found Polaris, the North Star. I drove slowly, cautiously, afraid of sinking into a mine shaft or soft sand, but the jeep sailed on, and took me all the way to the paved road. The Visitor Center parking lot was deserted. I hid the key fob under the mat, and with the hem of my dress, carefully wiped the wheel and every surface I had touched and climbed out. The Police would find it and return it to whoever had rented it. I walked back to the hotel. The lobby was empty. The front desk phone buzzed incessantly, the clerk had to be around somewhere, bathroom break maybe. I skirted the desk and grabbed my room key and sprinted for the stairs. The red phone light blinked steadily; the message told me the crew had finally arrived.

The shoot was to be tomorrow, I could meet them in the lobby first thing to go for an early morning breakfast. I ate an apple and banana from the complimentary fruit bowl, sank into a hot bath, and tried to wash the thorns and sand out of my hair. I slipped between cool sheets in the king size bed, and fell into a nightmare of ugly trees and deep holes.

It was still dark out as we ordered breakfast at the all-night diner. I hadn't mentioned to my colleagues I had been to hell and back. Any whiff of scandal, the tabloids would be all over it, the fickle sponsors would run like rabbits, the agency would be blacklisted, and my career would be over.

I was sipping coffee when the street door opened, and a large man walked in. He was wearing a Stetson and a red T-shirt with bold lettering on his belly, CHUBBY BUT SEXY. I lowered my head, trying to hide. He looked around the crowded café, searching for someone. He spotted me.

"Hey, silver Jeep!" he boomed, making his way to our table. All eyes swiveled to me. I busied myself stirring sweetener into my coffee. Undeterred, Cowboy bellowed, "Where's ya friend, I'd like to take him up on that ride!"

I looked down at my lap, my cheeks glowing hot. My table waited. The cowboy waited. I mumbled, "I'm not sure where he is." Mercifully, another voice rose above the din and a man standing across the room was waving his arms. The cowboy tipped his Stetson. "Well, I'll find your Marine at the Base!" he said and went to join his friend. I shrugged and said nothing, so my table went back to discussing the Los Angeles mix-up that had delayed them.

It was a tight fit in the van, the camera crew and their equipment, the makeup artist, the Director, the catered lunch, and several gallons of water. We passed through the Oasis of Mara entrance into the Park. The silver Jeep was still in the Visitor Center lot. The first pale fingers of light crept over the horizon as we pulled into a campground. Rimmed by magnificent towering boulders, windproof, sun proof, with spectacular rock formations, it was an ideal spot. All hands pitched in to get ready for the day's shoot.

Fall and Winter ad campaigns are always shot in the summer. That's fashion. It worked well for me that day. The long sleeves, high necks and sweeping ankle-length skirts hid my scrapes and bruises. The makeup woman knew better than to ask as she worked on my blotchy face.

To the southwest, the Little San Bernadino Mountain range was a pastel glow, the forbidding Berdoo Canyon a mere blurred crack. Birds called shrilly, and the aroma of the desert rose like sweet nectar from the warming sands. My spirits rose with the awakening sun. I felt lighthearted, my troubles slipping away with the layers of darkness. By the time the blistering noon heat engulfed the desert, the crew and I would be long gone, this place and its secrets forgotten.

The Director had just positioned me to model my first outfit. She was shouting, "Tilt your face more toward the sun," when something moving out in the desert caught my eye. I heard the Director, but I couldn't obey. I was fixated on the figure in the hazy scrub. A man was heading straight for us, walking slowly but steadily gaining ground.

As he drew closer, I could see that he wore Vietnam camo pants tucked into black boots, and he was carrying a small pink backpack.

NO REASON TO THINK OTHERWISE

His receptionist showed us in and the doctor greeted us with professional remoteness. Probably about 50 years old, and every year had clearly been a big one. He pointed at chairs, and my mother took the one nearest him. They were knee to knee. The air hung stale and humid. No breeze floated in the open window, only the street sounds of honking, a siren, the dull roar of traffic. Disjointed strains of The House of the Rising Sun blared suddenly from a passing car radio, then faded.

My mother was babbling, "We are a bit late, we were held up at the bank, there was a real long line, so …"

At the bank the woman with the clipboard had showed her teeth and said, "How is your day going so far?" I wanted to say it was great until now. Clipboard explained, "We have a new business model." I wanted to say, "Is it seven customers standing in line and three reps yakking and drinking coffee behind the counter, is that your new business model? And your job is to stand there with your clipboard?

Mother was still talking, her voice high-strung, brittle, a blend of her native New York and accents from below stairs at Downton Abbey. "I needed to cash her disability check, so I had to wait in line at the bank. And you're three flights up, those sure are steep stairs, I am all outta breath …"

Dr. White Coat leaned toward me. "How are we today?"

"Oh, she doesn't talk," my mother said quickly.

"Never?"

"Never." My mother said it firmly.

Dr. White Coat wrote something.

They always have to write something. What did he write, she doesn't talk, and her mother never stops?

"She was a slow baby."

Maybe because I was alone in my crib all day in an empty house, Dearest Mother?

"Slow developmentably," my mother added.

She has done the rounds of clinics and doctors and has heard that word, or something close to it, and she likes to use it a lot in case a new doc doesn't catch on right away.

Dr. White Coat didn't look up.

My mother added, "She's a Downy."

That caught his attention. His eyebrows went up. "But she doesn't look … she does have, but not so much …"

I can hear you, Dr. White Coat.

"Oh, yes, she is. She's a Downy."

The doctor was frowning, studying me closely as though I was some kind of alien specimen. I avoided his gaze and examined the framed certificates on the wall.

Dr. White Coat clamped his pen between his teeth and worked at rearranging his clipboard.

What is it with people and their clipboards?

"Has she always lived with you?" He was mumbling through the pen.

"Oh, yes, she's always lived with me," said Mother.

Bad choice, but no choice, Doc.

"I am her primary, and only. Sole provider."

I swear I heard a half-sob catch in her throat.

"Do you have any other family, in case, you know, anything should happen to you?"

"No," Mother said mournfully. "There's no-one."

Oh, get real, Dearest Mother, there's your sisters. And, let's face it, DM, you are the loudest, whiniest, most demanding, least talented, least good-looking of the bunch.

Dr. White Coat pressed on. "And, I have to ask, regarding support, there's no husband or father in the picture?"

"He died." My mother looked down at her hands, the bereaved widow.

Good side-step, DM. I remember when you bought yourself a wedding ring and wore it because of the neighbors, but never mentioned to me, nor have I ever seen, anyone called "husband." There has been a succession of greasy-faced male visitors, right, DM? But I don't think the doctor means those.

"How about nutrition." The doctor had his clipboard up and running again and was writing.

"Oh, she's very well-nutritioned. I am a very good cook," my mother assured him.

You mean the fried meat curled to shoe leather and veg boiled to tasteless mush, generously seasoned with your cigarette smoke, DM?

"And has she ever had anything removed, you know, appendix, tonsils, spleen, gall bladder?"

"No, she's got all her parts."

No thanks to you, DM. Don't think I don't know you inquired about having me sterilized. Yes, that's what I said. About three or four nurses back, and she was shocked and horrified. Me too. That was one step too far.

"Has she ever had any education?"

"Oh no, you can't do much with them, but I pay a woman to come in and work with her." My mother said it piously. Her sacrifices would definitely not go unnoticed.

Um, that would be the 12-year-old from downstairs. She does her homework at our apartment, and she shares what she learns with me. I was reading Dickens at 8. And I also switch to *PBS whenever you are out of the apartment. I can't stand Dora the Explorer.*

"Now, again I have to ask, but how was your marriage?" The good doctor was looking at my mother.

"Oh, abused women suffer in silence while their self-esteem erodes," she said.

DM got that from watching Dr. Phil. At this point I can no longer hold it in. I can hear myself disguising a laugh as a choking cough.

The doctor said sternly to me, "A mother often parents through unprocessed hurt and resentment. They offer love in different ways."

Well, you must watch Dr. Phil too, Dr. White Coat. But believe me, those weren't careless glancing blows of hers, those were deep mortal cuts meant to wound.

And then I winked at him. A great big, obvious wink.

There was a long pause. A long, long pause. The doctor looked down at his clipboard.

He finally looked up and said to my mother, "I think we need to schedule another visit. I'd like you both to come back, we'll run some tests. See my receptionist, she'll give you another appointment on your way out."

My mother's voice was shrill, her face red, her bulky chest heaving. "Come back? Come back for what? All I needed was your signature. Just one fucking signature, I mean, is that so hard?" That last was almost a screech, and she rummaged in her purse and pulled out a piece of paper.

"Just sign this, and I'll bring her back, I promise I will." Her hand trembled, the paper rustled. The traffic noise grew more strident, along with my mother's pleading voice. "Just sign it, doc! Otherwise, I won't be able to get a check for her."

Dr. White Coat took off his glasses and looked toward the window. "I am afraid I can't."

Well done, doc, you just earned all your certificates on the wall.

The receptionist closed the door behind us.

My mother struggled to return the paper to her purse, all the while inching toward the concrete steps going down. Her feet moved automatically as she muttered, "Now I've got to find another doctor ..."

I slid my toe forward, just the very end of my shoe really, and stopped it just in front of where she would take her next step. Her foot swung forward, met mine, and being top heavy, down she went.

She flopped over and over, the contents of her purse clattering out around her as she fell. I watched as she went down, down, down, her cries growing dimmer.

Doors opened, and people came onto their landings and leaned over the railing. Their faces looked down, and then up at me, and then down again at my mother.

I stood very still, watching people exclaim and press their hands to their mouths.

Now how do I could get across town to my mother's sisters. I am excited about starting my new life as part of one of their nice, normal, loving families, in one of their nice, normal, comfortable houses, with my nice, normal, smart cousins.

And then I heard people gasp, and I heard my mother groan, and then I saw my mother sit up, and then rise to her knees, and then grasp the stair rail, and then pull herself to her feet. She looked at me.

And all the people clapped, and turned their smiling faces up to me.

MISS YOU DARLING

Two hikers found the bones in a dry canyon creek bed. It sounds funny now, one said, but he thought it was a bunch of golf balls stuck in the sand. Just round white knobs, barely visible, protruding slightly, noticeable only as the dust blew away. Too big to belong to an animal, the hikers had to agree on that, they had seen plastic human skeletons in doctor's offices. They had discussed it, and they were of differing opinions: one wanted to continue the hike, after all the bones could have been there for months or even years, and the other wanted to return to civilization and report the bones immediately. The latter won the day, because the exuberance of their hike would have been dampened by the stain on their conscience of an unreported discovery of human bones.

The police at the nearest town were hardly lit on fire by the news. The bored desk officer slapped a form on the counter along with a No. 2 pencil stub, and the hikers tried to fill in the boxes. It didn't seem relevant to include their birth dates and race, but they did their civic duty and gave the information required. They left the building feeling disillusioned by the police officer's apathy, and neither any longer harbored hope that their ruined hike had achieved a good purpose.

What they didn't know is that during that year, 1980, California had 29,975 adult persons who simply walked away from their lives and were listed as voluntarily missing. And there was little optimism that a bunch of random bones out in the wilderness would lessen that number. Perhaps it isn't hard to understand the police officer's jaded outlook.

But luckily, there was a positive outcome. Even with the slim to miniscule amount of information given in the papers, somebody did claim the bones. There was more in the article about what else was found abandoned in the dry riverbed, the tires, a Safeway shopping cart, a mattress, and a child's car seat, than there was about the results of the police investigation into the bones. Perhaps that was because the police were playing their cards close to their bullet proof vests, or perhaps it was because they simply didn't have anything more to add.

The story of the bones was reported in the local paper, of course, but also a bit further afield because it happened to be a very slow news day. The article's meagre information was enough to catch the eye of one man, a man who had a very particular reason to be interested. The report hazarded a guess that the bones belonged to a roughly 50-year-old woman who had died of natural causes. And even though that was all it said, Mr. Hamilton Walker III leaped up from his Barcalounger Power Recliner, and in spite of the high price of gasoline, and the dry, stark, unimaginably monotonous sepia scenery, he drove miles inland to get to the police station.

To have a member of the public come in and so enthusiastically claim one of the missing, and take a Jane Doe off their books, well, all you can say is that it was a very welcome event. A solved case for them and a solved mystery for Mr. Walker. He was directed to the morgue, and the morgue directed him to a funeral home, and the formalities were completed. The bones showed no sign of foul play. There was mention of a slightly arthritic left knee and Mr. Walker readily agreed that Mrs. Walker had suffered such.

DNA would not be used to identify anyone for a few more years, but there seemed to be enough to release Mrs. Walker to her bereaved husband.

Mrs. Hamilton Walker III's funeral was justifiably solemn. There was a handsome casket upon which Mr. Walker placed a large bouquet of flowers and a tasteful cream envelope inscribed: *Miss You Darling*. Almost the entire population of the community tried to squeeze into the church. The full turnout might have been due to guilt that life in town had gone on unruffled without her, or perhaps relief that they could now stop tiptoeing on eggshells around Mr. Walker. Mr. Walker had occupied the family pew with a long miserable face every Sunday for months. He merely nodded at parishioners who offered their thoughts and prayers.

At the time, word of her disappearance had spread fast. The police gave statements to update the concerned residents. The chief of the detective division told them that this exclusive area with its multi-million-dollar homes on large, secluded lots is an inviting target.

He stated, "The houses are surrounded by thick privacy hedges and high walls, this could have been an abduction after an attempted burglary that was interrupted by Mrs. Walker." He sighed. "Or, then again, it might not."

Which didn't answer the question: where *was* Mrs. Walker?

The local paper headlined stories of abductions, human and otherwise. The ladies-who-lunch began to triple-lock their doors, alarm companies did a roaring trade, and high electric gates appeared at the end of every long winding driveway.

Discussions of the mystifying disappearance of Mrs. Walker took center stage at all social gatherings for quite a while. But then interest faded. Christmas was approaching, and houses were being decked in garish red and green lights, lawn flamingos in holly wreaths, and chimneys in the usual plastic Santas. Mr. Walker was persuaded to open his home to neighbors, just as Mrs. Walker always had in Christmases past. He had by far the largest home they pointed out, and they hinted that Mrs. Walker might be inspired to return for the festivities. Mr. Walker listlessly agreed and left them to it. The good ladies hired a professional decorator, of course, but they also bustled about decorating and embellishing an already over the top home, bringing in not one, not two, but three tall Christmas trees.

Guests were greeted at the door by Mr. Walker, and, to everyone's surprise, by a very young, very pretty helper, Bugsy. Bugsy wore a quite dazzling, unbecomingly short (they thought) silver sequined shift. She was bubbly and animated, taking her duties as substitute hostess quite to heart. Neighbors did look quite critically at her figure. She was 5 feet 2 inches and weighed around 100 pounds, probably a size 0, certainly not a 1, and much like Mrs. Walker, she favored glitzy attire and impossibly high heels.

The months had passed, and there continued to be no word from or about Mrs. Hamilton Walker III, and it was obvious that Mr. Hamilton Walker III needed to get on with his life. That was when the newspaper article about finding the desert bones appeared, and Mr. Walker was able to claim them as those of his wife.

It was quite a surprise when it came to everyone's attention by the third Sunday after the funeral that their neighbor and friend Mr. Walker had remarried. What's more, the supposed wedding took place at some "chapel" – the townspeople always made air quotes when they said it – in Las Vegas. Everyone was breathless to meet the new Mrs. Walker. They got their chance when the Walkers sent engraved invitations to friends, neighbors, and useful business associates for what they called an "intimate soirée."

The invitees were astounded to find that the new Mrs. Walker had already completely redecorated the big house. Not a stitch of the old Mrs. Walker's antique furniture and dark heavy appointments remained. It was now an art-deco haven, with modern prints and strange contemporary iron and wood shapes nailed to the walls. And the invitees were even more astounded to find the new Mrs. Walker was somebody they had already met; it was none other than the size 0 Bugsy. Well, the town said, men always do pick a replacement that resembles their ex.

And then the envelopes started coming. The first was handed to Mr. Walker as he exited his home one morning, about to leave for his office. He had one leg already in the limousine, when a breathless messenger bicycled up.

Mr. Walker absentmindedly gave the boy some change, all the while turning the envelope over in his fingers. He stood, one leg in, one leg out, staring at the envelope.

The chauffeur heard him say, "I don't understand, what does this mean?"

The messenger had long gone by the time Mr. Walker looked up. He stared down the driveway toward the gates as though expecting to see the messenger still there, waiting to be asked the obvious questions.

After a long silence, he said to the chauffeur, "I won't be going in today. You'll be paid for the trip of course, but I can't ..."

Nothing more came out of Mr. Walker's mouth, so the chauffeur stood waiting patiently for Mr. Walker to retrieve his leg so he could close the limousine door.

Mr. Walker continued to receive the mysterious envelopes. They arrived in the middle of the night inserted between the iron bars of his locked gate; they arrived stuck in the windshield of his 450 SL in the church parking lot; they arrived in his mailbox wedged between his bills and glossy magazine subscriptions. And the envelopes always contained the same thing: a receipt for a very expensive piece of clothing. That's all. Just the receipt. The clothes were all Rodeo Drive, pricey and chic. Balmain and Givenchy jackets, Comme des Garcons garish leather skirts, Gaultier Paris dresses, and all paid for in cash. When questioned, the salesgirls shrugged and claimed not to remember. There was a code of silence, wealthy patrons liked their privacy, or they would shop elsewhere.

But each tasteful cream envelope was addressed in his ex-wife's unmistakably precise hand: *Miss You Darling.* And with each one, Mr. Hamilton Walker III sank into his Barcalounger, face ashen.

NEW ENGLAND ARCHITECTURE

T he latest protest signs had not yet been ripped off the chain link fence. The site workers couldn't keep up with them. Local sentiment simmered against the tall ugly pastel concrete intrusion in their laid-back little beach town. Bad luck, bad timing, bad karma, bad judgement, you name it, not to mention an uncooperative local city planning board, all these had thrown the builder off his game. What's worse, he had just demolished an historic building to clear the lot, thinking if he did it quickly no-one would notice. The City noticed, and the City was not pleased. They came after him like the cavalry, guns blazing, with fines, liens, cease-and-desists, enough paperwork to choke a horse. They intended to smack him down and bury him along with all his crooked exploits.

Balding, with heavy jowls and long yellowed teeth, this squat bulldog of a man had financed a dozen projects just like this one around the state. During the economic recession, Jakub Grabowski had trodden on many toes as he voraciously swallowed up failing properties, ruthlessly crushed smaller competitors, snapping up their construction projects for cents on the dollar. His single-minded focus had cost him four wives, though to the women's chagrin, high-priced lawyers had managed to preserve his assets.

The car pulled through the gates, past the flapping protest signs, and made a compact arc into the empty parking lot opposite the building. Three concrete stories, sterile, angular, all sharp corners and flat planes, it had all the grace of an East European apartment block. It rose out of the hard packed dirt, looming large over the modest beach cottages that lined the street. Its garish pink, blue, and green paint was out of place among the surrounding quaint and tastefully designed custom homes.

Mr. Grabowski's car was not in the parking lot, and Edgar cursed nervously.

"Oh shit, he's not here. I need to call and let him know I'm here. Are we late? Why isn't he here?" Edgar got out and stood next to the open driver side door, digging in his pockets. Mary Sue unbuckled the twins and hoisted them out of their car seats. Another woman, Champagne, crawled slowly and with great difficulty from the cramped third back seat. She unfolded herself upright, and stood massaging aching limbs, looking about.

Edgar was frantically searching for his cell phone to announce his arrival. The sun glinted on his greased-back hair and on the perspiration that popped out on his forehead. Mary Sue was fussing with the twins. Champagne moved toward the building. Edgar glanced at her as she passed.

"You need a comb," he said.

The back seat breeze had done its worst. "New style," she said.

She moved swiftly past him. The whiff of his hair oil was nauseating.

She was aware that her short skirt showed off to perfection her tanned legs. She hoped the man they were to meet was watching. Little dust devils twirled around her Louboutins as she strode across the packed dirt. Gulls wheeled overhead, shrieking and cawing, prompting awareness of the ocean a short block away. She walked to a sign stuck in the ground by the steps. It said MODEL OPEN, and while it generally served its purpose, it was crooked. She bent to straighten it and glanced back at the car. Four-year-old Marli was squatting down examining stones in the dust, the net layers of her pink tutu billowing out around her. Mary Sue was racing after Chester as he sprinted for the gate. Edgar was groping around under the car seat, butt in the air. Champagne smiled to herself; if the owner was there inside somewhere, she'd have him all to herself for a few minutes.

The meeting with Grabowski was to be in the model unit kitchen, around the center island. Champagne stepped carefully over a pile of debris at the door. Cold, tasteless and sterile, the kitchen offered the cheapest materials, the lowest quality finishes, and the poorest workmanship. Linoleum floors were already cracking, laminate counters buckling, and the obviously discounted appliances were covered with dents and scratches. The painters had missed patches of the door trim, and raw wiring snaked out from holes in the walls. As Champagne wandered through the unit, she noticed the window louvers were installed upside down allowing the rain to pour in, glass sliders were installed back to front preventing insertion of a safety bar, and the master bedroom door was installed to swing outward instead of in.

It was fortunate that Champagne was standing in one of the few closets, looking for the missing clothes pole, when a roar shattered the silence. Even though she was sheltered, the force threw her to the ground. She had the presence of mind to slip out of her Louboutins so they wouldn't get scuffed, and then she ran. She made it to the car. Edgar wasn't looking at her. Indeed, he did not even ask if she was OK. He was gazing, open-mouthed, stricken and horrified at the flames now licking up, and threatening to engulf the second and third floors, and along with them, his dream of earning a substantial sales commission.

The explosion was big news because Mr. Grabowski was such a well-known, and heartily disliked developer. He aroused antagonism wherever he broke ground. Local communities fought hard to prevent his monstrosities from coming into their small picturesque and very expensive New England towns. News outlets picked up the story eagerly, delighted to have something juicy and controversial for a change. Amid the daily fillers of beach cleanup, I-95 traffic pileups, and New York City murders, here was something big and local. Reporters really got their teeth into it.

The explosion happened late one Friday afternoon. Local TV stations were on it in time for the 6 o'clock news. Reporters shoved their microphones under the noses of every passerby. Most had nothing at all to say, they were merely out walking their dog or on their way back from Safeway. It is possible that some of them may have elaborated a bit to extend their moment of fame. The reporters gobbled up whatever they heard and threw in some thoughts of their own, and soon rumor had it that there were huge injuries.

Champagne was sitting comfortably at home watching *The Price is Right.* She was well into a quart of Rocky Road, with her feet in fuzzy slippers propped up on a futon and a small Band-Aid plaster over her left eye, when a breathless news flash reported the explosion and fire and interrupted bidding on a turquoise couch. Champagne was surprised to hear that she was in the hospital with major burns, wrapped head to toe in bandages. On the air, the fire was attributed to faulty wiring. In the back room, well, it was attributed to the old real estate ploy: when you can't build and you can't sell, what else are ya gonna do …?

Champagne was back in the office the next day. She posed in front of the company sign, graciously answering reporter's questions, speaking glowingly of the wonderful quality of the damaged condominiums, no doubt soon to be repaired and ready for their lucky new occupants.

Edgar was hovering near the door, hoping to be interviewed too. Mary Sue, whose job it was to straighten his desk, his grammar, his office, his files, his appointments, and his personal life, bent down to straighten his tie. She was taller than Edgar. But then everyone was.

One of the Realtors looked over at him and remarked, "Edgar, you have a caterpillar on your lip."

"It's a moustache, Lonnie," Edgar said, stroking it affectionately. "It hasn't fully grown in yet."

The reporters left without a glance or a word to Edgar. He looked crushed. Lonnie said to Mary Sue, "They were probably turned off by the moustache."

"Oh, I think it looks cute," Mary Sue said.

Before Lonnie could make a snappy reply, the front door opened. "Look what just slithered in," he said instead.

A squat brooding man entered. Champagne timed her re-entry perfectly, smiling brilliantly. Mr. Grabowski's eye swiveled in her direction. He paused mid-step, and he smiled back. Well, it passed for a smile, only his lips moved. His pale eyes maintained a reptilian unblinking focus as he stepped into the conference room. Mary Sue was wringing her hands and Edgar was bowing from the waist as they followed him in. Mary Sue closed the door. Then she opened it again. Her thunderous scowl said it was not her choice, as she beckoned Champagne in to join them.

A couple of days later, when Champagne came back to the office after a grueling listing appointment, she looked drained and exhausted. The clients had thrown at her all kinds of objections: the company was not well known, it did not have a good track record, they had heard dicey things about its broker, Edgar. She was more than bushed.

Lonnie walked over with a tub of yoghurt in his hand. "Did you get the listing?"

"No."

Lonnie peered into his yogurt tub. "So, I heard that you slept with a client once to get a listing."

Champagne recoiled. "He tried to rape me! I was giving my presentation and he …"

Lonnie interrupted. "Yes, but did you get the listing."

"No. And my company fired me."

"Ah, yes, the infamous Yellow Jackets, the lethal downtown wasps." Lonnie turned his spoon over and licked it and pitched the yogurt tub into the trash.

Edgar's kids ran in. Mary Sue followed.

Lonnie put two fingers to his temple, pinkie extended, and said, "And they are here because …?"

"Because the new nanny quit."

Marli was standing on tiptoe, pulling papers out of Champagne's in-box. "I got to poop pretty soon," she said.

Edgar buzzed Champagne and his voice crackled over the intercom. "Come to my office and debrief me on the listing presentation."

Marli heard her father's voice and ran across the office shrieking, "Daddy, Daddy, I got to poop!"

Champagne dawdled, not eager to explain things to Edgar. "Where's their mother?" she asked Lonnie.

"Oh, Mother-of-the-Year Daphne?" He sniffed. "Daphne's probably shopping."

Chester was sitting on the floor stapling Edgar's business cards together. He was singing to himself. *"The wheels on the bus go round and round ..."*

Lonnie popped the top off another yoghurt. "Daphne and Edgar. A match made in Hustlers' Heaven. She thought he was successful, he thought she was rich."

Chester kicked it up an octave. *"The wheels on the bus go round and round, round and round..."*

Lonnie went on, "Real Estate's just not happening for Edgar. Ergo, he's stuck groveling in Grabowski's slime. Except now Grabowski doesn't have a building for Edgar to sell. No close, no rose. No sold, no gold. No honey, no ..."

"Money. I get it."

Chester's monotonous voice trailed across the room. *"Round and round, round and round."*

Champagne went to the supply room to be out of earshot of Chester's singing. Edgar followed, to be out of earshot of Mary Sue. He told Champagne that Grabowski wasn't happy with the company's lack of clout. He might be looking elsewhere for representation. Edgar wiped his forehead and said he needed Champagne to turn up the sex appeal and work on Grabowski. His voice was whiny. It's not clear what her reply was.

An inquiry came in, a buyer wanted to see a house for sale in town. Edgar took charge and made some phone calls. He came out of his office shrugging into his jacket, telling Champagne that they "could continue their discussion on the way." Mary Sue, who would be left behind to baby-sit the twins, was glowering dangerously.

They reached the house, and Champagne knocked, and then knocked again. Edgar stepped in front of her and retrieved the key from the lockbox and let them in.

Champagne said nervously, "The house is dark, they didn't leave any lights on. You set it up, right?"

"Well," Edgar said vaguely. "I couldn't reach anyone … but that probably means they're not home."

Champagne called out, "Agent! Agent!" No reply, the house was quiet. She set about turning on lights, and opening doors so the buyer could just walk in and view the rooms easily. She climbed the stairs and started opening bedroom doors. One room had an unmade bed, so she quickly bent and straightened it, and she put shoes away in the closet and clothes in a drawer. She moved swiftly down the hallway, straightening rugs, and even opening windows.

Edgar joined her. "Cool stuff," he said, peering enviously into the rooms.

Champagne opened the last bedroom door and froze. There were people in the bed. She quickly backed out, trying to block Edgar's view and close the door. Edgar could tell there was something he shouldn't see. He elbowed her aside.

"No, Edgar …"

Too late, Edgar flung the door open wide.

Edgar stood rooted to the spot, his mouth open. "Oh, shit, they're still here. And they're not going to leave." His voice was dripping disappointment. "They're too busy having sex."

Champagne had to grab Edgar's arm and literally tear him out of the doorway so she could close the door. Champagne had never moved down a flight of stairs so fast.

When they got outside, Champagne said to Edgar, "We need to head off the buyer. Quick, let me have her number."

Edgar dug in his pockets, pulling out scraps of crumpled paper. Champagne picked them up off the ground as they fell. Edgar couldn't find the required phone number.

Just then, a sleek forest green Jaguar pulled to the curb. Edgar ran toward the car, calling out gushing greetings. "Oh, right on time! So happy to meet you, come on in, it's all ready for you to see ..."

Champagne hissed, "Edgar, you can't!"

Edgar hissed back, "I have to get her inside, she won't buy it if she doesn't see it, will she. It will be Ok, we'll only show some of the rooms and ..."

The woman marched right past them into the house and in a high-pitched nasal New England voice, she started a running commentary. Champagne tried to dial her down a tad, but the woman liked what she saw and enthused loudly. Edgar eagerly encouraged her.

And then she headed for the stairs.

Nobody knows why she headed for *that* bedroom first. Edgar and Champagne stood looking on, horrified, as she flung open the door. She screamed, jumped back, pushed past Edgar and Champagne, and ran down the stairs and out the door as fast as she could. There were surprised screams from the bedroom. And there was Champagne standing there alone, mute, at the top of the stairs. Edgar had gone. He was running after his fleeing client.

Champagne said to Edgar, "What in the world were you thinking?" They were back at the office.

Edgar whined, "But I needed her to see that house! She wasn't going to buy it if she didn't see it, was she?"

Lonnie looked from one to the other. "So, why …?"

Champagne said, "It wasn't convenient for the sellers."

Edgar's face was red, his moustache twitched. "We only had to show the client the other rooms!"

Lonnie said wearily, "Will someone *please* explain."

"They were in bed," Champagne said. "Stacked vertically."

Mary Sue listened with interest. The twins had fallen asleep on the office carpet. Mary Sue took the opportunity to sneak into the conference room and make a call or two. Word circulated like a delirious brush fire that Champagne (Mary Sue didn't mention Edgar), had *insisted* on showing a client a house under such *inappropriate* circumstances.

Of course, Edgar had to fire her, he couldn't have his real estate company become a laughingstock. Mary Sue feigned tearful dismay when Champagne packed her desk plant and tape dispenser and marched out the door.

The State bought Mr. Grabowski's garish pink, blue and green condominium project, earmarking it for much-needed low-income housing. Mr. Grabowski was already breaking ground on another condominium complex a mile up the coast, intent on imposing his architecture on another charming New England town. Champagne had joined him, and together they worked on mapping out a strategy to defeat the local city planning board.

SOME ASSEMBLY REQUIRED

His voice had the rounded, softly nasal intonations of the Gulf state, though it was a mystery how a creature of such beauty could rise from the dank and fetid swamps of Louisiana. His skin had a luminous copper glow, his hair was beach sand blond, his eyes the color of a clear summer sky. And he had worked the gym hard for an exquisitely muscled, tight body. The bayou couldn't hold him.

When he came to Hollywood, he sent out a hundred headshots. That's what you did in the late 60s. And his phone immediately jangled, the agents couldn't talk fast enough. Right there on that first introductory call, he was offered lavish and liberal contracts with enticing sweeteners like a free convertible, an apartment, designer clothes.

And then they met him in person.

One appointment was typical of them all. The agent bustled into the room, gazing with visible eagerness at the head shots in his hand as he plopped down behind his desk.

"OK, Étienne Baptiste, am I pronouncing it right?" The agent was speed-reading the bio. "From Louisiana. Well, let's take a look at you, Étienne, stand up."

To which Étienne replied, "I am standing up."

There was nothing anyone could do. They pointed out that there aren't any actresses shorter than him, and they couldn't put him on a box in every shot. Étienne's movie career was over before it began.

Étienne was still impressed by his own good looks and gazed at himself reverentially in every mirror, but ambitions that required the concurrence of the paying public had withered, so Étienne did what everyone in Hollywood does. He found a hustle. And he bought generous shoe lifts.

His looks were his currency. His picture was on matchbook covers and in a big ad in every free throwaway paper that filled the racks and gutters of Sunset. "I can make you a star," it said. "You can be famous and earn millions as a movie star." The kids came from small-town Montana, Wyoming, Nebraska, Oklahoma. They came with the conviction that success in a school play or election as home-coming queen would make them the next tousled 60s sex kitten, the new Brigit Bardot, Julie Christie, Jane Fonda. When they hit town, they saw Étienne's ads, and Étienne welcomed them all. He hired a couple of make-up artists away from the studios and a cheap photographer who would take their picture, and for the $100 they had saved from part-time jobs at their hometown Dairy Queens and Burger Kings, and a percentage of their earnings, they were promised movie stardom.

I was one of those kids. I was tall and thin, and I had the requisite waist-length blond hair. But I had no cheek bones and a face all awkward hollows and angles no camera could love. So instead of promoting my movie career, Étienne married me. He was surrounded by people on pause, people who had no loyalties, people just waiting to flit to the next opportunity. He felt confident that I would stay. I was the Plain Jane with no illusions, and I was ideal for his purposes. We moved into a house in the Hollywood Hills. The attraction was that it was far from the gawking tourists but close enough to impress our clients that we were Hollywood players. And for a midwestern kid like me, the attraction was the orange tree in the garden.

I had always known Étienne had money problems. Vendors with strained faces would come to the door day and night. I would say he's not here and give them 3 minutes to whine before I closed the door. I took a waitressing job downtown. It kept us afloat and paid the bills. I helped Étienne in his business as well. We promised to circulate the kids' new headshots to all the studios. To accompany these photos, we wrote up a brief bio. That was my responsibility, to come up with something creative, something that would impress, something that would make a kid different from all the others. But their lives had so far been short and uneventful, where they came from was dull, and the kids were indistinguishable from one another.

Until Carter Cosi Smith.

She arrived with all her childlike farm-girl glow. She was slender, delicate, with milky skin and hair the color of the wheat fields and prairies she had just left behind. I was there on the Saturday that she came to us. Étienne watched her as she stepped into the room. He gasped at her achingly fragile beauty. He leaned in, he hovered, he studied her from every angle, as though searching desperately for flaws, anything that would render this amazing creature human. There were no flaws to be seen, none. And Étienne was clearly smitten.

I dutifully got to work on her bio. I searched for something that would make it out of the ordinary, trying to please Étienne by making it interesting, making it stand out from the usual stories of cheer leading, babysitting, church choir.

"Have you ever been abroad?" I asked.

"Yes," she said. "My parents took me to Alaska when I was little."

That conversation became a standing joke among Étienne's Lady Boys. Not Carter Cosi's reply, but my question.

"Have you ever been abroad?"

"Yes, and I am still a broad."

Patience, Prudence, Primrose, and Passion, they were Étienne's Lady Boys. I suppose he got the term from the American sailors in port in New Orleans, just back from Thailand. The Lady Boys danced in the Strip clubs. They were all about elaborate poses and exaggerated gestures and clashing perfumes. Here in our little house in the hills above Sunset Strip there was privacy, they could be themselves. They came with flaming red bouffant hair, green and blue glitter eyeshadow, purple or black lip gloss, and surgical enhancements beyond the imagination of nature. "Some assembly required," they declared, flaunting their new assets.

They had little use for me. I was there to straighten the couches they flopped onto, to bring them ice-cold drinks, to pick up the orange peels they tossed casually on the floor.

"Oh, do take my bio," they'd mock me, shrieking in unison, "Ask me if I have ever been abroad."

It was Étienne they wanted. They tried to outdo each other, talking in loud extravagant voices, jockeying for the spotlight, growing more strident, flouncing more noticeably, elbowing each other more sharply to get next to Étienne. He loved it, he loved being the central figure, the light around which these moths fluttered. He encouraged their outrageous antics, he played to them, and he identified with them. Like him they were beautiful to look at, but like him they were cast-offs, flawed, inadequate and incomplete, their beauty unacceptable to the larger society where it mattered most.

Étienne lured them to him on the pretext of arranging a Ball, just like the grand Louisiana Mardi Gras Balls he remembered from his childhood. He encouraged them to form krewes, plan themes, and begin to make their dazzling costumes. He in turn would locate a Ball site and arrange permits, he said, and deal with city rules.

But then he seemed to be preoccupied elsewhere. In those first heady days that Carter Cosi was with us, Étienne hovered possessively, leaning in when she spoke, touching the arm of her chair tentatively, as though to touch her flesh directly would burn his fingers. Around her he was always smiling, smiling, smiling. He seemed to start every sentence with, "Carter Cosi ..." He'd say it rapturously, his eyes sparkling, his lips curving around her name, savoring the words, rolling them on his tongue. She was an entity he had internalized, the force that drove his panache, his elan, his charisma. If I protested his distraction he would tell me quickly, applying just the right amount of innocent conviction, oh, she has potential, she'll make us a fortune, and then you can stop working.

At that point I think I knew that would never happen. The stop working part. I learned from some of the kids that not only were they paying a lot more than $100 for our services, but none of the cash was going into our bank account. I suspected then that it was going up Étienne's nose.

Étienne didn't invite Carter Cosi to the Lady Boy parties. It was as though he didn't want to sully her genteel mid-western sensibilities with baser tendencies. Besides, the

Lady Boys preferred to be with their own, they could let loose and go wild. When everyone was horizontal – drunk, stoned or otherwise engaged – I'd go up to the roof garden and look out over the city lights. Those were the moments when I could allow myself to cry, when I thought I would not be disturbed and not have to explain red eyes and swollen lids to anyone.

But one evening, Passion popped up beside me. Before I had a chance to dry my tears and wipe my nose, he sat down and patted my hand. "Hush, hush," he said comfortingly.

I mumbled vaguely of going home.

"You can't go home Dahling, you've seen too much," he said. "Buck up and apply more blush, that's what I do."

"Don't you ever want to just give up and go home?" I knew his struggles must be far more profound than mine.

"Oh, I let those small wounds just glance off my soul." He shrugged. "I endure. And you must too."

Ideas for the Ball had been bandied about for weeks, and Étienne's Lady Boys were eager for some action. A party was planned to discuss progress. The liquor store van pulled up, and the driver brought in cartons and set them in the entryway. He wiped perspiration from his forehead and paused. He didn't hand me the usual chit for signature.

"Um," he said awkwardly, "your account's gone way past due."

Étienne was in the kitchen. I called to him, "Étienne, did you hear? He needs cash."

"Then give him cash, Idiot," Étienne snapped irritably.

I said, "I can't, I don't have any money."

"Then just leave the booze and I'll pay next week."

The driver hesitated. "I'm sorry, I can't …"

"Then there won't be a party, will there." Étienne stormed into the bedroom, slamming the door. The lock made an abrupt click.

I apologized to the driver. With an audible expletive, he reloaded the cartons on his trolley and took them back to his truck. I called each of the Lady Boys to let them know the party was cancelled.

And there never was another.

I found a second job to support us, working evenings. I came home late one day, fatigued way beyond dog-tired, planning to ask Étienne to contribute more, to maybe get a real job. Carter Cosi was there, sitting close to Étienne on the couch. I looked at them together, and I felt like one of their discarded orange peels, used-up, unwanted and superfluous. I moved out the next day.

I ran into Passion at the Supermarket. He said to me, "Well, and then that happened."

"You must have known I would eventually leave him."

"Oh, Dahling, it's not that. It's just that you couldn't *possibly* compete. It was there right under your silly nose."

"What was, what am I missing?"

"Carter Cosi's a Lady Boy, Dahling. He got Étienne, and you and I didn't."

Fast forward 30 years. I was working morning shift at the Hollywood Café, sweeping up shards of a china plate, the handiwork of a truculent three-year-old. His mother was apologizing profusely to me as she guided her child's flailing hand to get toast into his mouth.

The door opened, letting in a rush of warm air. And there he was. He was stooped, his head jutted forward making him look shorter than I remembered. His hair was now a shock of brilliant silver, but there were still the same sky-blue eyes and copper skin, though a bit looser, the jawline less defined. Of course, I looked different by then too. I had never been a standout, but the long hair was now a short pixie, and my waistline had disappeared.

They took a window table and sat across from one another. I let my colleague serve them. I watched as Passion, considerably toned down now but still obviously Passion, reached across the table, and in a gesture so instinctive, so gentle, guided Étienne's shaking hand to his mouth.

So Passion did get Étienne after all.

ON THAT DAY IN JULY

I am writing today to tell you a story you need to know, my child. It is about my Russia, the homeland that I will never see again. We were in Yekaterinburg, at the foot of the Ural Mountains. The mountains rise like a girdle bounding the eastern rim of the Russian Plain. The highest peak, Mount Narodnaya, soars to just over 2,000 meters, but she stands alone among far more modest summits. Plateaus and ridges cut north-south across the austere landscape like a graceless, craggy spine slouching from the Kazakhstan border to the Arctic coast, and even beyond, if you count the archipelago of small islands extending out into the ocean.

Along the eastern slopes of the Ural Mountains lies the Sverdlovsk oblast, or region, which spreads from the crest-line to the West Siberian Plain. The soil is rich with ores, but too poor for agriculture, and almost the entire oblast is a swampy taiga of pine, larch and birch. It is here on the eastern slope that the mining town of Yekaterinburg stands, and just to its west, a narrow pass snakes through the mountains affording the main traffic route from Siberia into Europe.

It's not a large town, nor is it an old one, as European towns go. Named in honor of Catherine I, wife of Peter the Great, it lies along a tributary of the Tobol River, 1,670 kilometers east of Moscow. In the 1700s Yekaterinburg grew to importance as a mining town with an ironworks and a fort, and in the 1800s with the construction of the Great Siberian Highway, and the Trans-Siberian Railroad that runs right through the middle of the town. In the 1900s, the town pivoted once again into the public eye, this time with the execution of Tsar Nicholas II and his family. And that, my child, is the story that I need to tell you today.

I was 17 years old that summer. In Yekaterinburg, the summers are clear and warm. The clouds had parted, and the bright blue sky appeared like a delicate egg-shell dome, bathing the little town in buoyant light. The first blooms had already burst out into a brash spectacle, and birds were all atwitter in the hemlocks, scarlet maples and pines. But we were allowed to enjoy none of that. That was the summer our family was confined to the house on Voznesensky Lane. It was known as the Ipatiev House.

It was after the Revolution in October of 1917 that the Bolsheviks, or Reds as they were known, took control of Yekaterinburg. But the White Army was approaching, and the Bolsheviks feared defeat; they feared that the White Army would release Papa to reclaim the throne. Though I doubt Papa would have, indeed he hoped we would be exiled to live in peace in any country that would have us. When he was crowned in 1896, he was not trained to rule and frankly I have to tell you, my child, ruling did not become him. Papa had promised constitutional reforms after the first Russian Revolution in 1905 but went back on his word. He had agreed to a Duma, a representative assembly, but whenever the Duma opposed him, Papa simply dissolved it.

In 1914, Papa had led Russia into World War I to try to restore Russia to its former status as a great world power, and more importantly I suspect, to regain his dignity after the humiliating loss a decade earlier to the Japanese. Once again, it was an ill-advised war that Russia was ill-prepared to win. Our soldiers suffered devastating defeats at the hands of the Germans. Food was scarce and public discontent grew and led to mounting support for the revolutionary Bolsheviks. And it was no surprise that in 1917, revolution broke out on the streets of Petrograd, and Papa was eventually forced to abdicate his throne. That, my child, ended more than 300 years of Romanov rule.

The Bolsheviks brought us to Ipatiev House, which belonged to a mining engineer named Nickolai Ipatiev. Ipatiev didn't want to leave, but he had no choice, he was told the house was to be used for a "special purpose." The guards put up a wooden fence, so nobody could see us. We occupied the upper floor with some of the servants who had come with us, and the guards were all on the ground floor.

One night, the guards woke us, and tricked us into going down into the basement. They told us that it was for our own safety since the White Army was coming to fight the Bolsheviks for the city. It wasn't an earthen or stone basement, mind you, it wasn't cold or forbidding. It had a high plaster ceiling, beautifully carved arched wooden doors, and pretty striped floral wallpaper, and the wood floor was scrubbed clean. Not that we had ever been coddled at any of our own palaces. Even though we were Grand Duchesses, for some reason Papa had thought it prudent to raise us in a Spartan way. We slept on hard camp cots, took cold baths every morning, and we had to do chores.

Anyway, the basement was empty, so Mama demanded chairs, and the Bolshevik guards brought us two. The Tsarevich Alexei and Mama each took one. The guards came back in and asked to take our family portrait, just for historic value, they said. So again, we obliged them, and I and my sisters Olga, Tatyana and Maria arranged ourselves behind Alexei and Mama, and Papa stood kind of awkwardly in front. Of course, I realize now the photo was intended to be proof that every member of the family was there.

You can see in the picture that I was not the beauty of the family. Far from it. That title went to Olga. She had spun gold hair, striking blue eyes and porcelain white skin. It was said that I resembled my mother, and I did have her fair hair and light eyes, but also, unfortunately, I was short and fat with a pudding face and heavy dark eyebrows that met somewhere over my nose.

It was not just for my ungainly looks that I was a great disappointment to my parents. Or to my entire extended family, if you want to know. When I was born, Papa was so upset he had to go for a long walk to compose himself before he could go in and meet me. My aunt, the Grand Duchess Xenia Alexandrovna, is reported to have wailed, "My God! What a disappointment! A fourth girl!" Her cousin the Grand Duke Konstantin Konstantinovich cried, "Forgive us, Lord, if we all felt disappointment instead of joy. We were so hoping for a boy, and it's another daughter." Someone wrote later that when I was born Papa said he would have given half his empire if only for one Imperial boy. So that was not a good beginning for me.

And I did not redeem myself anytime later. I admit I was impossible. In fact, it was said that I held the household record for punishable misdeeds. One cousin declared, "Anastasia is evil and nasty." In one snowball fight I knocked poor Tatyana down by wrapping snow around a large rock. I cheated at games, I kicked and scratched opponents, I deliberately tripped the servants, I climbed trees and hid for hours. I had little interest in the school room, and I played pranks on the tutors. Our tutors said charitably that

I was lively and mischievous, when in fact I was rude and insensitive. They told Mama, "Anastasia is a gifted actress and can turn on the charm," meaning that I told lies well. But looking back, I think perhaps all those aggressive traits may have stood me in good stead for the tribulations to come.

Mama had an ally to help her with her children. She relied upon a Russian peasant, Grigori Rasputin, who she said was a holy man, though other people smirked and called him the "mad monk." Even Papa's sister Grand Duchess Xenia Alexandrovna said Rasputin was "sinister." He used to come into our nursery each night just as we were undressing for bed. He would pinch our bare bottoms and laugh as though it was all in good fun. Our governess, Sofia Ivanovna Tyutcheva was appalled. She complained, and was promptly fired. The Tsarina would hear none of it. Not long after, our other governess, Maria Ivanovna Vishnyakova, was raped by him, but again Mama refused to believe her story, and she too was dismissed. We knew better than to ever tell Mama anything against Rasputin because she was so fragile and sick with worry on account of the Tsarevich Alexei. Our little brother, Alexei, was a hemophiliac, and Rasputin had convinced Mama that he could cure him. We girls and our mother were all doubtless carriers of the hemophilia gene. Olga hemorrhaged during an operation to remove her tonsils and almost died. All four of us girls bled more than was normal.

Anyway, in 1918 the Bolsheviks were in control of most of Russia when they moved our family to the Ipatiev House in the town of Yekaterinburg. Rasputin had already been murdered by then, and a sailor, Alexei Nikolaevitch, carried our very weak little brother, Tsarevich Alexei, into the house in his arms.

The guards watched us constantly. They caught me poking out my tongue at them. One of them told everyone I was "offensive" and a "terrorist." But my sisters and I did help the cook make bread and we helped the cleaning women move the beds to scrub the floors, and we were able to whisper with them when the guards turned their backs. But we were there 73 days, and the tension of close confinement was beginning to take its toll. We even stopped singing our responses in the prayer services.

Out-manned and out-gunned, the Bolsheviks anticipated that the town would fall to the approaching anti-communist White Army. Our guards woke us on the night of July 16, 1918 and took us down to the basement. They posed us for our picture, as I said, and then left us.

Suddenly the guards came back in and told Papa that we were to be executed. Papa turned to us, making sounds of reassurance, and right then, he was killed by several bullets to the chest. Some of those bullets also killed Mama and Olga. Then more bullets followed, ricocheting off the walls, and hitting my sisters. So many guns were fired at once, and at such short range, that the room was filled with thick smoke. I had sewn my jewelry into my corsets, and the bullets could not pierce all those diamonds and rubies. Because I was so short, as the smoke filled the room, I was able to crouch down unseen. One of Mama's maids, Anna Demidova, was next to me. I heard her groan, she had survived the bullets, so the soldiers came over and bayoneted her. I was covered in her blood. There was so much blood, it clogged my nose and filled my eyes. I was sliding in the blood, and I fell to the ground, and the others fell on top. I remember little after that. I probably fainted.

When I awoke, I was in a grave underneath all the bodies. They had buried us just 19 kilometers from the city, in the muddy Porosenkov Ravine, in the Koptyaki Forest. I could hear the guards shouting that with the bodies out of the truck, they could maybe now pull it free. It seems they had intended to take us to the copper mines, when they became mired in the mud. I heard Anna Demidova groan again, and again the guards had to bayonet her before they threw her in on top of me. The guards poured sulfuric acid on us, some of it trickled down onto my arms, and I bit my tongue not to cry out. Then they hastily shoveled dirt onto us.

I waited and listened for a long time. I was forced to move when lack of air made me dizzy. It was a surprisingly shallow grave; they had been in a great hurry, throwing us into this makeshift hole instead of taking us to the mines. They had placed some thin railroad sleepers on top of the loose dirt, but I was able to easily crawl out. I put it all carefully back in place, so that if they returned, they wouldn't know that one of us had got out. I stumbled into the woods and washed myself, watching the brackish pool turned crimson. Other than the sulfuric acid burns, I was unharmed, none of the blood was mine.

White Army soldiers helped me escape, and my je is paid my passage across the mountains. I arrived in Paris, just another one of thousands of Russian emigres fleeing the Bolsheviks. Your grandfather was a successful French businessman, a good man, and we had a good marriage. He once asked about the burns on my arms. I said a cook had accidentally spilled hot grease on me.

Eventually there were suspicions that I might have got away. There was the right number of bodies in the grave, and Demidova was at first thought to be me. But she was much taller, and rumors of my escape grew. So of course, there have been imposters, at least ten that I know of. One of them, Anna Anderson, said she had feigned death among the bodies of her family and servants, just as I had, but she looked nothing like me, and she couldn't speak a word of Russian. There were others, all largely ridiculed, and so will you be. The Reds will hound you like the jackals they are. They have already murdered 84 members of our family.

But I have thought long and hard, and I decided I must give you the choice. It has been 70 years. Your mother is gone, I am old, and I too will soon be gone. You, my darling grandchild, will be the only one who knows what happened on that day in July. And it is your choice. You can fight them to claim your rightful place as heiress to the Romanov line, or you can keep your secret and take it with you to the grave.